MOST
WANTED

ALSO BY BRADLEY WRIGHT

Alexander King

THE SECRET WEAPON

COLD WAR

MOST WANTED

POWER MOVE

Alexander King Prequels

WHISKEY & ROSES

VANQUISH

KING'S RANSOM

KING'S REIGN

SCOURGE

Lawson Raines

WHEN THE MAN COMES AROUND

SHOOTING STAR

Saint Nick

SAINT NICK

SAINT NICK 2

MOST
WANTED

Bradley Wright/King's Ransom Publishing
www.bradleywrightauthor.com

MOST WANTED/ Bradley Wright. -- 1st ed.
ISBN - 978-0-9973926-9-2

For John Younce
I've had the good fortune of meeting many a fine gentleman in my life. But you, sir, stood above them all.

"That was the trouble with lies: it was very important to remember them accurately when, generally, they were the things you most wanted to forget."

— LIZA CODY

"Running away will never make you free."

— BARTON GELLMAN

MOST
WANTED

1

There was a chill in the air as Alexander King leaned against the corner of the high-rise building. Night had fallen over Mexico City. The weather reminded him of San Diego. The underbelly of crime, however, did not. Across the street, the drug-lord-turned-human-trafficker whom King had been waiting for exited his black Mercedes sedan. The streets were mostly quiet. Not uncommon for two in the morning on a Thursday night. Especially when the party section of the city was a couple of blocks away.

King took a step back behind the brick wall to further conceal himself. He'd been in Mexico City watching Raúl Ortega for the past three days. Learning his patterns, studying his habits. The man was infamous in all circles of intelligence across the globe, but especially in North America. His reputation was that of a ruthless leader, quick to silence detractors by any means necessary. For over a decade it had been all about drugs. However, for the last year his operation had grown into pedaling humans. The reason King was watching was because young American girls had become his choice of sale.

So far King had learned one important thing: Ortega was never alone. This didn't surprise King. Men like Ortega always have someone hunting for their head. However, it seemed to King that Ortega had either grown complacent or he considered himself untouchable. Three days had shown King the man wasn't afraid to be in public. He'd visited night clubs, restaurants, and even outdoor markets. Anyone with any sort of skill wouldn't have a problem removing this drug king from his throne. That's why it frustrated King that for the first time in his career as an assassin for the CIA, he had only been sent there to gather intel.

He hadn't been sent in to kill.

The entire thing had been odd to him. What was the point of learning an enemy's patterns if you weren't to capitalize on them? Sam, his longtime partner and a handler at the CIA, thought the same thing. So much so that she'd almost told him to stay in the Cayman Islands with the new woman in his life—Cali—but Director Lucas was adamant it had to be King. So there he was, watching a known kingpin go about his normal routine, only to report on it, not to stop it. Meanwhile, Cali was in bed all by herself on the other side of town. He could still be with her in the islands, overlooking the beach, but instead they were stuck in the city where neither of them wanted to be.

Consequences of the job, he supposed—never getting to go where he wanted to go. All he could hope was that his legwork would somehow help nail this criminal in the future.

King took one more glance toward Ortega's car. When he did, King's entire operation changed. Under the bright glow of a streetlight, he saw one of Ortega's men pushing a Caucasian female out in front of him. He could hear her cry of distress from a block away. There was no way King could just sit back and take notes after his eyes witnessed what was almost certainly a woman being taken against her will, being forced into only God knew what next.

King pulled his phone from his pocket and dialed Sam.

"Everything all right?" Sam answered. Her British accent sounded sleepy. He must have woken her.

"No. Ortega has a girl, and she did not want to be with him."

"I won't ask you how you know this for a fact," Sam said as she cleared her throat. "But I will tell you it doesn't matter. This is a strict no-contact operation. Do not engage, X."

"Easy for you to say, Sam. You didn't hear the fear in her voice as she was pushed into a building."

Sam was quiet.

There was the faint rush of traffic in the distance. The occasional horn honking, even a siren far away, but all of it was background noise to the sound of blood rushing between King's ears as his adrenaline surged and his heart rate quickened.

"Sam? No comments?" he asked her.

"Comments? No. Just lying here wondering why you called me. You and I both know that whatever I say, it won't change anything. You're going to do what you want to do. Next time just save yourself the minutes to wake me up, and skip the call."

Sam didn't sound frustrated, merely confident that what she was saying was true. And King had nothing to say in return, because he knew she was right.

3

"Just know," Sam said, "if it gets messy, the agency will deny to the Mexican government that you're one of ours."

"Then I guess you'll just have to come down and bail me out yourself."

"Wouldn't be the first time," Sam said. "Tell me why again is it that we work for the CIA? If you're constantly going to defy their orders, shouldn't we just go back to our own team and let them contract us if they'd like? We could go back to using your own plane, and you'd get to see your family and poor Kyle."

"How 'bout I just keep this clean, then we can worry about leaving the CIA on our own terms if we want."

"Not sure that's how it works, X, but whatever you say. Just be careful. This guy isn't a small-timer. He has an army at his beck and call, and probably half the Mexican government as well. Play the long game. I know you want to save the girl, but maybe you can save hundreds of girls if you wait and we do this right."

Sam, ever the voice of reason. He knew she was right; he just didn't know if it was in him to watch them take that girl.

Sam added, "Sometimes being smart is a better skill than being a magnificent killer."

King took a deep breath to slow his climbing heart rate. "Sounds boring, but I hear you. I'll be in touch."

2

The next morning Alexander King's coffee tasted sour. There wasn't anything wrong with it; it was the exact same coffee he'd had the last few mornings. The difference, he supposed, was the horrible taste he already had in his mouth from his sickened stomach after leaving that girl alone with those monsters last night. Every ounce of his being wanted to charge in there like he always did. He just couldn't. It wasn't about defying orders from the CIA, like Sam had said on the phone; he did that all the time. But he wouldn't have been able to get her out of there without getting her hurt, or worse. He had no backup in Mexico City, and it would have been much more than a one-man job.

But that didn't mean he liked it.

King watched the sun begin to rise behind the buildings across the street through the slit in the curtains of the hotel room. He hadn't slept a wink, but he did manage not to wake Cali. They had an early morning ahead. Their flight to Alaska was leaving soon. King was going to fly back with her and stay for a couple of days while he had a hole in his schedule. He wasn't too happy about going back to Barrow after what happened there only a short time ago—plus, it was still cold as hell there—but Cali would be able to keep him warm.

King felt Cali's arms wrap around his waist and her kiss on the back of his neck.

"Good morning," Cali said. "I didn't hear you come in last night. Everything go okay?"

King turned and accepted the kiss she was offering. The green in her hazel eyes sparkled in the morning light coming in over his shoulder.

"It was fine."

She squeezed him. "You excited to get back to the cold?" Her smile was ornery. She knew how much he hated it.

"Oh yeah, can't wait," he said, devoid of enthusiasm.

"Well, I'm going to hop in the shower. Join me?"

"Go ahead. Let me finish my coffee here and make a phone call."

Cali squinted her eyes as she stared up at him. "Hmm. Declining a shower with me. That's a first. You sure everything's okay? It's fine if it's not, you know. I do realize that every day doesn't begin with roses and end with champagne."

King liked Cali. He was probably already in love with her. But he wasn't ready to deep dive into feelings with her. At least not about the underworld in which he had to operate.

"It's fine, I promise. Just an off morning."

"Well . . ." She leaned in and kissed him softly on the cheek, then on the neck as she pulled away. "You're allowed those, I suppose. Just don't make a habit of it."

She walked away toward the shower. It was hard not to follow. She was only wearing a pair of tiny white panties. A man can't fake it when other things are on his mind. And as beautiful as Cali was, and as good as she would feel against his skin, his mind was on the haunting decision of leaving that girl alone last night. It was absolutely eating him alive.

King finished his coffee, and Cali, her shower. The two of them packed their things and loaded up the rental car.

"You want to stop and get some breakfast or just grab something at the airport?" Cali asked.

King put the car in drive and pulled away from the front of the hotel. "I'm okay to wait."

"We can stop and grab snacks too. Half the price of the ones at the airport."

"That's okay," he said. "I'm not much of a snacker."

"Yeah . . ." Cali patted his hand. "That one package of Fritos or M&M's might ruin your six-pack. I wouldn't be able to sleep with you if that happened. So, good thinking."

He didn't throw her a playful laugh as he normally would have. She patted him again, this time without speaking. She didn't know him very well yet, but Cali was a quick study and wasn't only focused on herself. She could tell he was trying to work something out in his mind, so she let him.

The thing his brain was working on now was the same as in the hotel room. However, they were now driving past the corner where he stood and watched that innocent girl be taken inside the lion's den, and all he could do was fester on how he'd let it happen. As they passed the entrance to Ortega's place, King made up his mind that he just couldn't leave Mexico City without at least trying to save her. All other orders be damned.

King took out his phone and pressed Sam Harrison's contact.

"No news of mayhem in Mexico City this morning," Sam answered. "You must have actually shown restraint."

"I did, but I'm not leaving." King glanced over at Cali. She didn't react. "I need you in Mexico City ASAP. Get Zhanna here, too, if you can. And I don't want to hear it."

"Hear what?" Sam said. "I'm actually proud of you. At least you're waiting long enough to get some help."

"Can you be here by tonight?"

"Don't see why not. Let me make arrangements."

"Don't tell Director Lucas." Robert Lucas was the director of the CIA. King knew he wouldn't be happy about King changing plans. As always, King believed in asking forgiveness, not permission.

"You don't say," Sam said, playing it up. "Seriously, though, Xander. When this one is over, there is no use for working for the CIA anymore. You never do what they ask anyway."

The airport exit was coming up on his right.

"Let's worry about the girl for now. I have to get Cali to her plane. I'll see you tonight."

King ended the call and immediately addressed Cali. "Sorry. I know we planned on going back to—"

"Don't apologize to me, Alexander. I knew who you were when I decided to travel with you. You don't owe me anything. Sounds like someone is in trouble. Save them, then worry about seeing me again."

King gave a thankful smile. "I will see you again, right?"

Cali leaned over as King pulled into short-term parking, in the parking garage just across from the airport's entrance.

She gave him a long kiss. "I certainly hope so, Mr. Special Agent."

"You know, I'm not just a piece of meat," King teased.

"Yeah, you are."

They both got out of the car. King left his bag in the backseat, but he grabbed Cali's for her.

"I'll walk you in. It's the least I can do."

"Not necessary. I'll be just fine."

"I want to," he said. "Besides, I have to run in and extend the car rental. It will be easier than calling since I'm already here."

Cali hooked her arm in his. "All right then. Lead the way."

3

───────

King strolled across the walkway back to the parking garage. It was hard to watch Cali leave. The two of them had shared a fantastic couple of weeks. It was the most fun he'd had in a long time. He could still taste her cherry ChapStick as he rode the elevator up to the level where his car was parked. It took longer than he wanted at the rental counter. There was a line of impatient travelers waiting to get their vacation started. Unfortunately, he didn't have his phone to pass the time; he'd left it in the car when he went in with Cali. Too many things on one's mind makes it easy to forget the little things.

King unlocked the rental and took a seat behind the wheel. He had a few hours to kill before Sam would be arriving. For the moment he was content to watch a few planes take off and land in the distance. His mind drifted from the task at hand—rescuing the girl from the grip of Raúl Ortega—all the way to the people in his life he had been missing desperately in the two years since he faked his own death to keep them safe. Sam had obtained a few photos of his niece, Kaley . . . she was getting so big. King missed hugging her and, of course, giving his sister a hard time for no reason. They were the only blood family he had left.

Then there was Kyle. They may not actually be blood related, but Kyle was his brother nonetheless. He missed getting into girl trouble with him. Sam said he was doing well. He'd been on assignment with the CIA in several different locations. Sam mentioned he'd acquired quite a few skills, but the most impressive she'd heard about was his ability to blend in while undercover. He was no longer the rookie King was teaching a few years ago. King longed to see his friend's growth for himself.

His thoughts led him back to Sam's suggestion on the phone last night. She'd mentioned they should go back to their vigilante team on several occasions. The only reason King hadn't made the move to do so was his relationship with the president, and the promise King had made him. He'd vowed he would always be there to fight for the United States when the president needed him. King had no interest in going back on that promise; however, his mind was beginning to shift to the possibility of having his cake and eating it too. To come back to life, so to speak, and bring his team back with him. Taking mercenary missions, but also being available anytime the president needed him. King wasn't sure the two could coexist, but it was a thought he was beginning to fall in love with.

Aside from the people he missed from his former life, he missed his home in Kentucky. He missed his horses and being a part of the races. He missed the thrill of seeing them thunder down the track for a win. More simply, he missed living a life. His life. As selfless as King had been to give it all up, it was beginning to take its toll. Meeting Cali only exacerbated that feeling because he wanted to show her who he really was, aside from the human hunter he had become. She had awoken a side of him that had been lying dormant since the night he met Natalie Rockwell. He was falling in love with Cali, and it was dampening his desire to remain living in the shadows. King was at a point now where the people who had threatened his friends and family were all dead. They had been the reason he had to disappear. Maybe now he could at least partially return to his old reality. And though he didn't want to get ahead of himself, these thoughts of living an actual life while still fighting for his country were exciting.

King's trance was broken by the buzzing of his phone that rattled in the console's cup holder. It was Sam.

"You on your way?"

"What the hell is going on down there, Xander?"

King's glowing mood instantly shifted to anxiety as he sat up in his seat.

"What are you talking about?"

"I've called twenty times in the last half hour. I thought you were leaving the Raúl Ortega deal alone until I arrived?"

"I was walking Cali into the airport and left my phone in the car," King said. "And what do you mean about Ortega? I haven't done a thing."

"We've got serious problems. I have to be quick. The CIA stopped me from getting on the plane. They're walking toward me right now, and they're going to take my phone. You're all over the news. I know you didn't do this, but you're going to have to find a way to prove you didn't. You have to run. They'll be on you there in no time."

"Sam? What the—"

"Just listen!" Sam shouted. "Do what I tell you in this order. Drive to a back alley somewhere, check your trunk, then search for yourself on Google. Do not text me back. They will have my phone. Break your phone and leave it in the alley. Pick up your go bag at our designated spot and disappear until I, or someone you know, gets ahold of you. Do you understand?"

"Sam? What happened?"

"I can't—" There was some rustling on her end of the phone. Then she shouted, "Just do what I said!"

The line went dead.

Sam isn't one for games, and when she was urgent about something, King knew it was serious. So as much as he wanted to Google himself, and as much as he wanted to check his trunk, he denied his urges, started the car, threw it in reverse, then slammed it into drive and pushed the pedal to the floor. The tires squealed over top of the concrete, and just as he was going out the one-way exit, the flashing lights of several police cars were entering the parking garage on the other side of the partition.

A million thoughts were running through King's head. The first of which: was Cali safe on her plane? The second was, what the hell could have happened that was so bad they stopped Sam from getting on a plane to come to him? As he drove back toward the city, he dialed Cali.

"Hey, miss me already?" she said.

"Are you on the plane?"

"Just boarded, everything okay? You sound stressed."

"It's fine. I'm going to have to lose this phone. I'll contact you from a burner. Fly safe."

King ended the call. He was worried the police would also be checking the plane for him, but then he remembered that the ticket was still under the cover Sam had given him in the Cayman Islands. Sam specifically said to Google *himself*, so that meant *Alexander King* was all over the news.

A supposed dead man.

King didn't know what was going on, but it seemed as though he was going to have to work fast as hell to figure it out.

4

King did his best to follow all traffic rules so as not to stand out. He remembered that the zoo wasn't much farther than around the corner from the airport. It wouldn't be very busy there yet, and he didn't figure many police officers would be patrolling that area. Besides, his rental car might be known to them, so it was more important to get somewhere quick and start figuring out what was going on than to stay out on the road —exposed.

King exited and followed the signs to the zoo. The public parking area had a gate that was closed, so he continued past it. Only a quarter mile ahead, he spotted an entrance for a public pool. There was no gate, so he turned that way. He drove forward to the pool's parking area. It was mostly empty, just a couple of cars near the entrance. He pulled to a stop at the far end of the parking lot. He had 360 degrees of good sight lines. No one was going to sneak up on him.

Though he could hardly wait to look for the news about

him online, he had to open the trunk first. A lot of things were running through his mind as he exited the car. If there was a news story, and the CIA was blocking Sam from coming down to Mexico City, he clearly had been framed for something. But what? Was there a bomb in his trunk? Some stolen weapons? Drugs? None of these things made sense for making national news. And that made him nervous.

King stepped up to the trunk and pressed the button on the keypad. It popped open a little. The sun was shining bright, and the day was beginning to heat up, but that had nothing to do with why his palms were sweating. He couldn't help but think what he saw next was going to change his life dramatically in some way. Maybe it already had.

He lifted the trunk and slammed it back down immediately. It was his visceral reaction. He scanned the area around him to make sure no one was coming; then he lifted it once again. There was a porcelain-skinned, brown-haired girl lying there with her eyes closed. Her hands and feet were bound with rope, and she had a gag in her mouth. King's fingers shot forward and checked for a pulse. He let out a sigh of relief when he found one. At least she wasn't dead. She was in a pink tank top, sweat stains at the armpits, and a pair of white shorts that landed halfway down her thighs. She looked young, maybe seventeen or so.

King's fears were correct: this was going to change his life. He had no idea who she was, but she had to be someone important for national news to be covering it. And though he didn't know what the coverage was about, he was sure it somehow incriminated him for her being there. It was the only thing that made sense. King reached down, untied the rag from behind her neck, and pulled it from her mouth. He walked around the car, opened the passenger door, and laid the seat back. Then he lifted her out of the trunk and placed her in the front seat. He did his best to check her entire body for any sort of tracking device without violating her. It was a fine line.

The girl was lifeless. It was obvious to King that she'd been drugged. That was the reason she was alive without waking up. But he checked her arm anyway just to confirm it. The red injection point was easy to see on her almost translucent skin. King shut the door and walked around to the driver's side. His mind was in a million places, but all he was trying to do was focus on the next best step. The area was still clear, but King knew that in the age of technology, they would quickly camera-track his car to the zoo.

The obvious thing would be to call Director Lucas and let him know he had the girl. However, given that Sam was being cut off as his go-through contact, it was clear even Lucas doubted King's innocence. Which meant that whatever evidence the news was airing must somehow be 100 percent incriminating. Otherwise, Director Lucas would never believe King would do such a thing. With the police already after him in Mexico City, King's best guess was that this was the daughter of someone *very* important. And they would soon be all over his current location via the cell phone in his pocket. He needed information; then he needed his go bag so he could disappear until he could figure a few more things out.

King got inside the car and opened his phone. He went to the Google app and searched his name. There were links to several related videos, most from the days he was frequenting the Kentucky Derby with his horses. But one stood out to him immediately. The thumbnail photo beside the video link was what looked like a car in a parking garage. The CNN link read "Dead Secret Agent Returns to Kidnap Senator's Daughter."

A few years ago King wouldn't have been worried about the video at all. He knew he hadn't kidnapped the girl, so the video wouldn't show absolute evidence. But in 2021 everything was different. Technology was on a scary new level, and videos called "deep fakes" were beginning to pop up everywhere. These deep fakes were videos that were so well doctored, you could put Richard Nixon's face on Tom Brady's body, and you couldn't tell the difference whether it was the former president giving a post-game speech or Brady himself. And King knew before he ever even pushed play, that was what this was going to be. He just hoped it wasn't the best fake he'd ever seen.

When King tapped the video, it filled his phone's screen.

He knew immediately he was in the worst sort of trouble. It was only a six-second clip, but someone had made it look unmistakably like he was stuffing the same girl he'd just taken out of there into his trunk. It looked so real, in fact, that he had to search his memory just to make sure he wasn't drugged and hadn't done it without knowing. He paused the video when his fake self was looking over at the camera right after he slammed the trunk shut. Even though it wasn't possible, it was unmistakably King's own face looking toward the camera. The way whoever had done this edited the video, it was clear they wanted people to be sure it was Alexander King.

That's why Director Lucas was cutting him off from Sam. This video was irrefutable evidence that King had kidnapped the girl. No matter how much King knew it wasn't true, none of it mattered. He was James Bond here in Mexico City. The cover he'd made Sam give him just for fun didn't seem all that funny now. Regardless, King couldn't prove he wasn't in that video. So the only way out of this entire thing would be to find the people who'd made the fake—and prove they did.

King had never felt so lost. Everything he'd ever done as a Special Operator, and as one of the CIA's secret weapons, had always had long odds. But as he sat there in the front seat of that car, looking down at video evidence of himself committing a horrible crime and knowing the world tended to work from a "perception is reality" mind-set, he'd never felt more defeated.

That's when he heard sirens in the distance.

The walls were closing in.

The entire world was coming for him.

5
———

K ing threw the car in drive and spun the wheels as he sped forward. He reached over and managed to get a seat belt around the girl. He circled the car 180 degrees and floored the gas pedal. Three police cars had already made the turn toward the public pool. King didn't try to go around them; he simply kept the pedal down and steered right for him. He would use the only information he was sure they had about him to their weakness. He had the girl, so the police would be forced to proceed with caution.

King wouldn't.

In a high-speed game of chicken, King steered right for the police car in front. The police had no choice but to part ways in front of him. King's rented Toyota wasn't exactly fast, but if he could get some distance between him and the police now, he might be able to disappear long enough to stop for his go bag. The phone, cash, and extra passport with a new identity inside would be crucial in the coming days. The extra Glock 19, spare magazines, and his Chris

Reeve Sebenza knife wouldn't hurt either. He had to treat the situation like he was going to war because from the looks of it, this might be the battle of his life.

King jerked the steering wheel left and changed roads as he tossed his cell phone out the window. They'd tracked it long enough. Just a couple hundred feet more and he swerved right onto the freeway on-ramp and plowed forward. He checked his rearview, and so far they hadn't caught up to him. He turned right to take the next exit, hoping to throw the police off his scent. Without a map or his phone for GPS, he was going to have to feel his way back to his go bag. Sam always had a go bag sent to wherever he would be spending even a little bit of time. Whether his stay was for business or pleasure, she'd never failed to do so. This time Sam had the go bag mailed to the FedEx store on Avenida Patriotismo. One reason she chose that street was because she thought the name was very apropos. The second reason was because she knew he wouldn't forget the name of that road. Though King didn't find her little "joke" as funny as she had, at least she was right. He hadn't forgotten. Now he just had to find that road.

Either the temperature was getting hotter outside, or he was just on fire inside, but he was sweating right through his T-shirt. He bumped up the air conditioning and made some turns in what he thought was the direction of the FedEx store. The only thing Sam mentioned about Avenida Patriotismo was that it was close to the hotel. He'd have to work to find it from there. But he was going to have to do that very carefully, because that area would be on high alert for him since he'd been staying at the hotel. He wasn't sure who knew what, so he had to assume his pursuers knew everything.

For the moment he'd lost the police cars. As he drove through the busy streets of Mexico City, he knew that one of his next priorities would have to be acquiring a different car. As he made his way toward the hotel, he scouted the area looking for potential marks. Having to carry the girl to the car he was about to steal was going to make things more difficult. Whoever he took it from was going to see her and then relay that to the police, eventually blowing his cover with that car too. But it would at least give him enough time to get his bag and put some distance between himself and the law.

King spotted a small grocery store and turned into the parking lot. He crept down the lane, spotting a car pulling into a space. He was happy to see that it was a man driving. King didn't want to hurt anyone, least of all a woman. He put his turn signal on like all was normal and pulled his rental to a stop. As the man shut off his car and opened his door, King pulled his knife and his pistol from the glove box. He'd stashed them there because he couldn't take them into the airport. He then exited his car, opened the back door, and stepped toward the man who looked to be somewhere in his fifties.

"Señor?" King called out.

The man turned toward him.

"Tengo un problema," King said as he pointed back at his car. It was one of the few things he knew in Spanish.

The man looked over King's shoulder at the rental car, but before he could respond, King already had an iron grip around the man's left wrist and the back of his shirt. The man's car keys dropped out of his hands. King moved quickly enough that the surprise kept the man from putting up a fight. A couple of steps later, King stuffed him into the backseat of the rental car and shut the door. The man found his voice and began screaming in panic. King reached over to the door and hit the lock button. Then he reached across the console, undid the girl's seat belt, exited the car, then pulled her out the driver-side door. When he shut the door, the man's shouting was muffled. King glanced around the parking lot and found that no one had really noticed. The street noise behind him had obscured a lot of the commotion.

King reached down and picked up the keys to his new silver Hyundai Elantra. Then he went around and gently placed the girl back into the same position as before: seat belt on, lying on her side. He took one last look around. Not a lot of people in the parking lot. The block down the road looked familiar; he knew the hotel was just around the corner. The man was pounding on the rear passenger door of the rental car. King got in his Elantra and pulled out of the parking lot. He was a ghost again. For the moment, at least.

King turned left, then eyed the street signs as he passed through intersections, until he finally found Avenida Patriotismo. A few blocks down on his right, he saw the familiar FedEx sign and breathed a sigh of relief. Step one in the million it was going to take to clear his name was in his sights. His only hope was that the next few steps would go just as clean.

He had no doubt they wouldn't. Nothing was easy, especially when a man is on the run.

6

"You can't keep me here, Robert," Sam said to Director Lucas. "You're treating me as if I'm some sort of prisoner!"

Sam Harrison's sharp British accent cut through the chatter in the break lounge at CIA headquarters in Langley, Virginia. The large room was filled with a few couches, a couple of round dining tables, and two agents placed there to watch her.

The dark-haired, fifty-year-old Director Lucas stared at her with a determined look. "Sam, you're in a break room. You're hardly being treated like a prisoner."

"Then I'm free to go?"

"Just look at this from my perspective, Sam."

Sam placed her hands on her hips—defiant, but listening.

"There is concrete video evidence that King put Senator Terry McKinley's daughter in the trunk of his rental car and drove off. Until we find him, I can't let you contact him. In the eyes of the law you are already an accomplice for giving him a heads-up before we took your phone."

Sam took a deep breath. She was trying to hold back, but she was seething. No one person had done more to protect the United States of America in the last decade than Alexander King. It was insulting—no matter the evidence —that Director Lucas was considering this. Thinking about it made her boil over.

"The law? Are you serious?" Sam jabbed her finger in Lucas's direction. "All the things you have us do for you that is outside the law, and you want to tell me by law I'm an accomplice? To what? A complete farce? You *know* X would never do this!"

"I understand where you're coming from, Sam. But no matter what I do or don't believe about King, I have to do this the right way. One of the most important men in this county is missing a daughter, and I watched King take her with my own eyes."

"Robert, this is not 1997. You know full well how deep fake videos work, and how excellent their quality can be. Video evidence no longer means a thing."

"Okay, Sam. I just need you to contact him, and tell him to come in. And to bring Brittany McKinley back safely with him. King ran from the police a moment ago. How does that not make him guilty."

"Don't play stupid with me, Director Lucas. You know he can't just come in with evidence that you believe of him taking her. Come on! He'll have to clear his name first, or no one else will. He's easily expendable because he's not even supposed to exist."

"First off, watch how you talk to me."

Sam scoffed and rolled her eyes.

"Second, if he's innocent, he needs to bring her in. He knows we'll find who did this if he didn't."

"Bullshit!" Sam had reached capacity. "Need I remind you what happened when a few years back, then Director of the CIA, William Manning, was trying to have Xander killed? Do you not remember that? Well, X does. So forgive all of us if at the moment there is no one for him to trust."

Director Lucas took a deep breath and walked a circle in thought before returning back to her. "Listen, I get it. Just call him, tell him to drop the girl so one of ours can pick her up—"

"You do not get it at all, Robert. Xander doesn't know who he can trust. So he certainly isn't going to chance that the innocent girl he's been stuck with gets put in the wrong hands. You—you're acting like you've never been in these situations before. You know how this works and how Xander operates. What is going on?"

Just then the door to the break room busted inward.

"Is this your traitor, Robert?" A silver-haired man with a red face and a three-piece suit came walking toward them. "Her and her scumbag double agent who has my daughter?"

Sam's blood pressure rose to a record level. She nearly knocked Director Lucas over trying to get to the man in the suit. It was one thing to call her a traitor, but calling King a scumbag double agent wasn't going to fly, no matter who this man was.

"You'd better watch your mouth!" Sam felt herself being pulled backward. The two agents had moved in to make sure things didn't get physical.

"And she's not even American?" the man said. "I should've known! Where's my daughter?"

Director Lucas stepped in between them. He looked back and gave Sam the evil eye. She knew then why Robert was being different about this case. Senator McKinley must have been applying a tremendous amount of pressure. That was evident by the senator's personal trip to Langley just to see Robert.

"Senator McKinley, no one here is a traitor. I told you not to come down here and that we were handling this."

"Handling this? Is that a joke? My daughter got stuffed in the trunk of a car in a foreign country, and you don't know where the man who did it is. Is that how you're *handling* it?"

Robert looked up at his agents. "Please take Sam to my office. I'll be there shortly."

The agents nodded and tugged at Sam.

"Wait a moment," Sam said. She wasn't very good at the soft approach, but she would do anything for Xander, so she was going to give it a try.

Robert nodded for them to wait.

Sam cleared her throat. "Senator McKinley, I presume?"

The red in the man's face had subsided a bit. He nodded to her without words.

"I understand this all must be devastating. I can't even imagine. But I assure you, even though it doesn't seem like it, you are actually fortunate in this situation right now."

McKinley bowed up his chest. "Fortunate? Are you kidding me?!" He looked at Director Lucas. "She serious?"

Sam answered before Director Lucas could. "Your daughter is in the hands of someone who would die before he let her get hurt. I don't know how or why it happened this way, but I promise you that is the case."

"Tell me where he is right now!" McKinley shouted.

"I know as much as you," Sam said, walking toward the door. The agents quickly followed. "He's somewhere in Mexico City. If the entire world hadn't been called to attention, and the world police hadn't taken a stance against him, you would already have your daughter back." Sam peered at Director Lucas. "But since they have, X has no choice but to stay hidden. You've pushed him into those shadows. Now you'll have to wait until he's ready to come out."

"Bullshit, Robert." McKinley turned the conversation back to Director Lucas. "King used his passport to enter the country from Mexico City into John Wayne Airport in Orange County, California, two days ago. The next time he showed up was that video from Mexico City a couple of hours ago. It's him. And if you don't want to find him, that's fine. I'm already on it."

"What the hell is that supposed to mean?" Robert said.

Sam stood in shock as Senator McKinley stared at Director Lucas. She couldn't believe her ears that Xander's passport had been used in California. "Robert," she interrupted, "Xander isn't even traveling under his own passport. Hasn't for over two years. You know this, and you know why. This is some sort of setup."

"Both of you, quiet for a moment." Robert looked at McKinley. "Sam's right, Alexander King would never have used his own passport. And how did you even know that? If you have information you aren't sharing . . . Senator, this is serious. You can't keep information from us."

"You are the CIA, Robert. How do you not already know what I know?"

"Because you've apparently gotten a head start and hired someone else. Who the hell is it? And where the hell are they? Tell me now or we have an even bigger problem."

"This is my daughter!" McKinley took two steps forward and stuck his finger in Director Lucas's face. "I'll do whatever I need to do to get her back. Whatever it takes!"

"Not from jail you won't." Director Lucas took a step back, then took a deep breath to let himself cool off. "I'm sorry, sir, but there are a lot of things at play here. You have to give me all the information you have. And I need it now. You might be putting an innocent agent *and* your daughter in even more danger."

Senator McKinley took a breath and relaxed his stance. He looked over at Sam, then back to Robert. Sam knew she had heard all she was going to hear.

Director Lucas took the hint. "Sam, please wait in my office. I'll be right with you, and we'll start to sort this out."

"Okay. But I have to say this," she said to McKinley. "If you've hired someone, you need to tell me. You're only adding danger to your daughter's situation. X will take care of her. But not if he doesn't know who's after him."

"Yeah?" The Senator's look turned arrogant. "We'll see about that."

7

King drove about a mile away from the FedEx store before pulling over into an alley. There were some delivery trucks unloading restaurant supplies just up ahead, but for the most part he was alone. He checked the pulse of the girl beside him. She had been out for quite some time, and he wanted to make sure his situation hadn't gone from bad to worse. Her heart was still beating. He couldn't really make a good next move until she came to and filled him in on all of her important information.

The sun was at full blast now, but the shadows in the alley made him feel a little better about taking a moment to make sure he had what he needed. He chose this alley in particular because it was right next to a convenient store that he hoped would have a backup burner phone to purchase. But he couldn't do it himself. The cameras would all be watching for him now, so that was another reason he needed the girl conscious.

He unzipped the black backpack he'd picked up at

FedEx and began rummaging through it. He pulled out the Glock 19 and the spare magazine and set them on the floor of the car. He took out the ball cap and put it on. It was always good for more cover. He pocketed the spare Chris Reeve Sebenza framelock knife and then pulled out his new passport. It was American, and his fresh identity was Thomas Crown. He chuckled as he knew it was one of Sam's favorite movies but also her play back at him for his last identity request of James Bond. There were several other goodies inside, and after he pulled out the burner phone, his hand found the last things at the bottom. Two airline bottles of bourbon. Sam always put them inside the go bag for him. Her way of saying hello in his native tongue. He would save them for later when hopefully he could enjoy them.

King opened the burner phone and powered it on. Normally there was nothing on the phone but the contact information for Sam's current burner. However, this time, when it powered up, he had a text message.

"That's a first," he said aloud.

King pressed the button opening the message. It was from Sam. She'd thought ahead before she'd called him with her other phone earlier. And this message might just prove to be a lifesaver.

As soon as you input these numbers into your new burner phone you're going to go get right now, get rid of this one. They'll be combing this phone and a message was sent to your number. So toss it. If you don't already know, the girl they say you've kidnapped is California Senator Terry McKinley's daughter. I wish I had more info, but just learning about this didn't give me time. If I can't help you, call Dbie first thing. I'm leaving current contact info with her for our former Team Reign members. Hope-

fully one of them can help. X, I'll be doing all I can to find out who has set you up, but I'm not sure Director Lucas will let me get away with anything. I'm calling you right now. They are already here to make sure I'm not helping you. Call Dbie from the new burner. Her phone will not be traceable. She's your only lifeline. 555-245-2112.

King closed the text message, entered Dbie's phone number, and pressed call. Dbie Johnson was his and Sam's resident tech wizard. She wasn't on CIA payroll, or anyone else's, for that matter. Sam had been paying her full-time money under the table to be ready for just such an instance. Dbie was their best-kept secret.

"Sam?" Dbie answered.

"No, it's X."

"X! How come you never call me when you're not in trouble?"

"Perks of your job, I guess. Can you fill me in?"

Dbie went right in. "Brittany McKinley was taken from a nightclub in Orange County, California, two days ago. Her friend's statement to the police was that one minute they were partying and the next she woke up on the floor of some abandoned house, Brittany nowhere in sight."

"Any video around the nightclub show anything?" King said.

"The police are being tight lipped, so I hacked the DVR of the nightclub's camera system. I just finished combing through it. I couldn't see where the two girls were drugged, but the place was packed. And there was a huge fight, so it muddied everything. I found them staggering out into a black sedan. I'm getting ready to run the plates, but I'd bet everything I've got that the car was stolen."

"Why?"

"Well, if whoever is doing this is good enough to make a video showing you putting her in your trunk when you didn't actually do it, and using your passport at John Wayne Airport, they probably didn't miss that detail on the car."

King was in shock. "Wait, what? My passport? As in Alexander King?"

"Yep. The ghost of clandestine past is back, and everyone in America—well, the world—knows you're alive."

"But it wasn't me."

"But it *was* you to the millions who've watched the now-trending video and are following the story. This is a conspiracy theorist's dream, X. People are eating this agent-come-back-to-life story up. Especially since you were in the public eye so much at the Kentucky Derby a few years back."

Even as Dbie said it, he felt as though it was someone else who'd lived that life. It seemed as if it was a hundred years ago when he'd had the freedoms of civilian life.

"Shit," King said.

"Yeah, that's what I said. That video is good too. Done by a real pro. If I didn't know you, I would totally think you were guilty."

"Thanks, Dbie."

"You got it," she said, matching his sarcasm. "What should we do now?"

"When's the last time you talked to Sam?"

"I was on the phone with her as she was typing the text to your burner phone. I didn't call her back. I trashed that burner she called me on. I knew the CIA would be going through it. She said she'd call if she could, but that was a while ago. I'm assuming she's been locked down."

"Whose contacts did Sam send you?" King asked.

"Zhanna and Jack. Then she said 'contact only in extreme emergency' when she gave me the number for a guy named Patrick O'Connor and your old buddy Kyle."

King pulled the phone away from his ear for a moment. Hearing Kyle's name as a potential contact shook him. His oldest friend in the world still didn't know he was alive. King knew Sam said "contact only in extreme emergency" because Kyle, and Patrick, for that matter, were both still employed by the CIA. He swallowed his emotion and put the phone back to his ear.

"X?"

"Yeah, I'm here. Did you contact Zhanna and Jack?"

"I did. Zhanna is booking a flight to Mexico City in case she can help. Jack didn't believe me when I told him you were alive. He was pretty rude. After I told him that you actually are alive, and under fire in Mexico City, he just said, 'Bullshit,' and hung up on me. I called him back but he didn't answer."

"All right, well, I imagine it was quite a shock for him to hear I was alive after two years of believing otherwise. At least Zhanna is on the way."

"I'll relay burner numbers to her as we go."

"Thanks, Dbie. Let me get my new burner and I'll call you back."

"Roger that. My new burner is the same as this number, but 2113 at the end. I'll trash this one. Talk soon."

King ended the call, and right when he set the phone in his lap, Brittany took a deep inhale in the seat beside him. She was finally awake.

8

King couldn't get a word out before the shocked and disoriented girl's instincts kicked in and she began swinging at him. He tried to be gentle with her, but she was like a feral cat cornered in an alley. He caught both of her wrists and held her arms still.

"I'm not going to hurt you. I'm here to help."

With her arms useless, she swiveled her butt in the seat, leaned back, and swung her legs around. She got in a couple of good kicks to his chest before he was able to pin her legs down against the center console.

"I don't want to hurt you. But you have to calm down. I'm undercover CIA. I'm not your enemy. I need your help."

Brittany fought against King's strength for another few seconds before she finally gave in.

"I know you're scared, but I'm on your side."

"Why should I believe you?" Brittany shouted.

"Because you're not still bound, gagged, and lying in my trunk."

Brittany was quiet for a moment. King continued to hold her down as he still felt the fight moving through her.

"Can you please let me go?" she said.

"Can you please not kick me anymore?"

King felt the tension fall from her limbs, and he slowly released the pressure he was holding on them. She tucked her arms and legs into a sitting fetal position as her eyes searched her surroundings.

"Who are you? Where are we? And how did I get here?"

King was blunt, "Thomas Crown. An alley in Mexico City. And I found you drugged and passed out in my trunk."

Brittany's eyes were wide. King gave her a minute to process. The food truck ahead of them in the alley was all but unloaded by that time. The bustle around them hadn't changed, and for the moment no one cared they were there.

"Tell me everything," King said. "It's the only way we have a chance at making it out of this alive."

"You just expect me to trust you? I wake up in some stranger's car who says he's undercover CIA so you don't have to show me an ID. Then you tell me your name is the same as one of my mom's favorite movies? You have a pistol at your feet on the floorboard, and you're built more like a soldier than any agent I've seen, and I've seen plenty around my dad. They're all skinny and pretentious. You're more action-figure and normal. So don't be surprised if I don't open up right away Mister Whatever-your-name-is."

King was taken aback. He knew very little about Brittany, but his read on her before she'd awoken was that she was probably a spoiled little rich girl with very little in the street-smarts department. But she was quite the opposite. Intuitive, observant, and good at reading people, not the normal traits of a senator's daughter.

"Okay. Very good. Someone in your family a cop?" King said.

Brittany rubbed at the track marks on her arm from being drugged. "No. But I've been babysitting for this private investigator who used to be FBI. He always tries to teach me something new every time I'm over."

"It's working. You're very observant."

"Yeah? Well, not observant enough. I'm here, am I not?"

King nodded. "Yeah, but don't be too hard on yourself. The world is full of people meaner than you are smart. Always will be."

"You one of them?" Brittany turned toward him and looked him in the eye.

"Yes," King said. Brittany looked surprised. "But I'm only mean to people like the ones who took you. I told you, you're safe with me."

Brittany ran her hand through her dark hair and sucked in a deep breath. "Okay. But if that's true, can we start over? You telling me the truth this time?"

King gave his surroundings a once-over. There was no reason not to be honest. He was already on blast throughout the entire world as taking her via the fabricated video. Hopefully it would help her open up.

King looked back to her and extended his hand. "Alexander King."

Brittany reached out and shook his hand.

"I used to be a Navy SEAL, so your soldier take was dead-on. And speaking of dead, only a handful of people knew I was alive until a couple of hours ago. I've been a ghost working with the CIA for the last two years."

"What happened a couple of hours ago?"

"A video of me putting you in the trunk began circulating all over the national news. Now I'm the most wanted man in the world."

"Yikes. And I thought I was in a bad spot." A slight grin grew on Brittany's face.

"I know, right?" King played along. Brittany was a surprise. She was nothing like his preconceived notion. That didn't happen a lot in his line of work. "Jokes aside, you okay?"

"Depends. Did you really put me in the trunk of this car?"

"The video is pretty clear."

"Yeah, well, video in 2021 is a lot different than it used to be. You have kind eyes, Mr. King. You don't seem the type to want to kidnap a senator's daughter. Besides, you look nothing like the guy who drugged me and my friend at the bar. And you don't seem to be the type who would be working for a Mexican drug lord, or whatever the hell the guy was who held me hostage in his penthouse last night."

"That was you?" He'd let the words slip before he could stop himself.

Brittany instinctively moved back against the car door away from him. She looked scared—confused. "So it *was* you?"

"No, sorry. That's not what I meant. I am on a recon mission, and I saw you last night being dragged into the building."

"Oh, that's comforting." Now she was angry. "So you just, what, left me there to die?"

That stung King more than she would ever know. It was what ate him alive last night, and it was the reason he hadn't gotten on that plane with Cali. He was going back to get her. But she wasn't going to understand that. Not now.

"It's complicated." It was the best he could do.

Brittany's hand shot for the door handle, but it was locked. She moved for the unlock button, but King shot his finger down on lock, keeping her in.

"Let me go!"

"Brittany, stop screaming."

"Let me out of this car! Help!"

That shout was at the top of her lungs, and the two men loading boxes of lettuce onto their dollies at the truck in front of them both looked King's way. King started the car and threw it in drive.

"Help me!" she shouted again as he pulled forward down the alley.

The delivery men had a clear look inside the vehicle at King and Brittany. They would be able to corroborate with the local police that she was in his possession and under duress. This would only further sink him with Director Lucas and every other agency personnel who might be looking for him when word of it made it back to the States. And it would make it back. News travels faster than the speed of light anymore. If there was a shred of hope the CIA might still believe in him, it was officially dead.

As King drove past the delivery truck and out into the street, Brittany took advantage of the moment and unlocked the door. She was hanging halfway out before King could get hold of the back of her shorts. He swerved to miss a parked car as he pulled her back inside. He wheeled around a slow-moving truck, and the door slammed back shut. He put the steering wheel in between his knees to steer as he reached over Brittany and pulled the seat belt around her. He held it in place as he let go of her shorts and retook the steering wheel with his left hand.

39

"Stop fighting me! I'm here to help you!"

"Like you did last night? You let them take me, then I magically end up in your trunk?"

She struggled against the seat belt, so he pulled tighter.

"You're hurting me!"

"Stop fighting me, Brittany. Please."

"Why? You gonna hit me?"

King swerved around another vehicle, then settled back into his lane. "I'm not going to hit you. Just stop fighting or you're going to get us both killed." He nodded toward the road.

"Let me go!"

"Are you going to calm down?"

"Yes, now let me go!"

King locked the doors and depressed the child-lock feature. Then he let go of her seat belt. Brittany huffed and turned straight in her seat. King checked his rearview mirror to make sure no police had just seen his reckless driving. There were no police, but a car did catch his eye as it swerved in behind him two cars back. King checked his side mirror hoping it was paranoia, but the way the car was maneuvering, he didn't think it was.

"Do you know if they put a tracker on you?" King asked.

"What? Who?"

"The people who took you, or the man who held you captive last night. Do you know if they put a tracker on you?"

"Tracker?" Brittany sat up, worried. "No, I-I don't think so, why? What's wrong?"

"Put your seat belt on. Someone is following us."

9

"Do you have any idea who it was?" Brittany asked.

After a couple of miles and several circles around the same part of the city, King was able to lose the tail he'd had by swerving into a parking garage.

"No. I was hoping you might be able to tell me."

"Me?" Brittany said.

"Yes. I need to know everything that happened to you from the time of the kidnapping to when you woke up in this car. Everything you can remember. I have to stop being reactive, and the only way to do that is to figure out who I'm going after. Or at least figure out who is after us."

"I have no idea who that could've been. But I thought you knew who had me last night? Remember, you left me for dead?"

That sentence was like nails on a chalkboard for King. "I told you. It's complicated. Now start from when you were at the club two nights ago and go from there."

"There isn't much really . . . Look, I'm really thirsty. I don't remember the last time I had water."

"I'll get you some, just give me this info so I can get moving on what I do best."

"What's that? Kidnapping innocent young girls?"

King nodded. "Okay. You're scared and confused. I get it. But continuing to worry about me being the bad guy is only going to make it harder for me to keep you safe. Now, you're not dead or hurt right now, are you?"

"No."

"And you've been with me for a couple of hours, right? Have I made a call for a ransom or tried to hurt you in any way?"

"Well, no. But—"

"Okay then. Until you have a reason not to, I need you to trust me. We are both in a bad spot, but I promise you it could be worse. And it will be if I don't get things moving in our direction."

Brittany fiddled with the watch on her arm. "Okay. Fine. But just promise you won't hurt me?"

"I promise."

Whether or not in Brittany's mind it was an empty promise, it seemed to ease her mind, at least a little. For the moment.

"Cathy and I were in a bar in Orange County."

King raised an eyebrow. "You're seventeen, right?"

Brittany's mouth jerked up on one side as she shot him a "come on, bro" look. King smirked and rolled his hand forward telling her to proceed.

"We had just ordered our second drink when this super cute guy came over and started talking to us. I mean, he was way too old for us, but a total hottie. He had the most beautiful green eyes. Anyway, he was talking about being on leave from the Navy, which made Cathy's wildest dreams about to come true. She totally has the hots for men in uniform. Calls them barrel-chested freedom fighters. Anyway, his name was Scott, and when he showed her a picture of himself in his sailor's hat, Cathy melted. It didn't even matter to her that he'd lost his index finger in combat. It was just a nub. Didn't matter to Cathy, though. When I say she loves a man in uniform, it's, like, out of control. I mean, one time—"

"Brittany?" King interrupted.

Brittany finally took a breath. "Right, anyway, the two of them were really hitting it off. I didn't have anyone, but I was really happy for her because she had just gone through a *brutal* breakup. So she deserved some fun. But then these two Mexican men bumped into us, and Scott totally got into a fight with them. Like, a real-life street fight. The bouncers kicked all of them out, and Cathy was sad. That's when both of us realized we were way more drunk than we should have been after only two drinks, so we called an Uber. The last thing I remember that night was getting in the Uber and two men were in the front seat. Which I remember thinking, two Uber people was weird, but I was too out of it to care."

"Were the two men Mexican, do you remember?"

Brittany closed her eyes. "You know, they might have been."

King nodded. "Then what?"

"Then I woke up in the back of a van. I had no idea where I was. I was gagged and tied up, so I couldn't even scream for help. I passed out again. The next thing I remember was waking up in the back of a car. I think it was last night, but I have no idea how long I'd been out. More Mexican men pulled me out of the car. It was dark, and I

43

was in a city I didn't recognize. They said something to this well-dressed guy in a suit and pushed me into a building."

"Yeah, that was last night. I saw you."

Brittany gave him a cold stare.

"Did you hear anyone say this well-dressed man's name?" King asked.

"I remember them putting a shot in my arm once they dragged me inside some room. They thought I was out already, but I heard one of them call the man in the suit Mr. Ortega. Next thing I knew, I was waking up beside you in this car."

King was quiet for a moment as he thought through her recount of the last two days. There wasn't much, but at least he was able to confirm that it was in fact Ortega who had taken Brittany. He was pretty sure before that it had been her he'd seen last night at Ortega's place, but her story made him certain. It wasn't much, but at least he had a starting point. One of the most dangerous men in the world. What else was new?

"What are we going to do now?" Brittany asked.

The answer wasn't simple. King had a lot to wade through before he would be able to get Brittany to safety. He had no idea whom he could trust. If he didn't know there was a fake video of him kidnapping Brittany circulating in world news, it would be simple. He'd find a safe place to take Brittany, like the US Embassy, then go track down Ortega. But why would Ortega take a senator's daughter and try to frame King? As far as King knew, Ortega didn't even know King existed. So setting up a plot to get King caught made no sense. There had to be someone else involved. Someone who not only knew about King but wanted to make King look like a criminal.

None of the few dots King had at that moment were connecting. He needed more information. Ortega was the only lead he had, so that would have to be where he would start. But King was in a foreign country, with no resources, and zero allies. Not to mention an innocent girl he had to keep safe. All while avoiding any sort of law enforcement, including whoever the hell it was who was following him just a few minutes ago.

"Anything?" Brittany said.

King shook his train of thought and looked at Brittany. "First we need to get you some food and water and some clothes. And I need a new phone. You up for some shopping at the local convenient store?"

"I'd rather be at Bloomingdales, but I guess it is what it is."

"Yep. Unfortunately, it is."

10

King searched several rows of cars in the parking garage before finding an open door. It was an older car, so he was able to hot-wire it. He and Brittany took the back exit, and a few blocks over he found a convenient store. He knew changing cars wouldn't necessarily throw off his tail if the person following them was watching the garage exits, but it was better than not changing anything. He had given Brittany his hat and some cash and sent her inside for supplies. He didn't like letting her out of his sight, but he had no choice. King knew by then that all the cameras would be looking for him, and so too would citizens who'd seen his picture on the news.

While he had a moment to himself, he used his burner phone one last time before Brittany brought out some new ones.

"X, you really need to switch out this phone," Dbie answered.

"I know. I am. But this can't wait. I need everything you can find on Raúl Ortega."

"Raúl Ortega. Got it. Anything else?"

"Comb the cameras at John Wayne Airport. I need to know who used my passport, if at all possible."

"I'll find out what flight your passport was used on and try to match it up with video. But I'm not sure I can get into the airport's system."

"I have faith in you. Anything else?"

"The car Brittany got into outside the nightclub was stolen. So no help there."

"Glad you brought that up," King said. "One more thing. Zero in on who got into the fight. See if we can ID any of them. Brittany said she was talking to the white guy who got into it with two Mexican men."

"So, look up the Mexican men?"

"Might as well look them all up while you're at it. No stone unturned. She said the white guy's name was Scott, but if he's involved, it's probably an alias."

"Got it. I'll email what I find."

"Thanks, Dbie. Any word from Zhanna? She make her flight okay?"

"Haven't heard anything, so hopefully so. You'll know when I know."

"Good."

King ended the call, then broke the burner phone in half. He gave a look all around the car. No sign of the tail. And no sign of Brittany coming back out of the store. He was parked across the street looking directly at the side of the store. He chose this store because he could see both the front and back doors from his vantage point. That was when she finally came walking out. King scanned the area again, his hand on his pistol just in case.

Brittany opened the car door.

"What took so long?" King said.

Brittany handed him a bag with phones in it, keeping the one with food and water for herself. She squared her shoulders and looked him in the eye. "Because I was trying to decide if I should run or not."

"Okay. At least you're honest."

"I just watched you put me in the trunk of a car on a TV that was on behind the counter. Then your picture and mine flashed up on the screen."

"Why *didn't* you run?" King studied her face as he watched her remove his hat. Her brown eyes were determined. Her pale skin was flawless, unharmed by the passing of time and too much sun. Which surprised him a bit with her being from Orange County.

"Well, I was about to, but the video was on loop. I didn't catch it the second time through, but the third, it was pretty clear to me." She reached over and picked up his arm. Then she took his hand in hers, put it into a fist, leaving only his thumb sticking out. "Subungual hematoma," she said.

She was talking about the blood that had been trapped under his thumbnail since he was in Alaska. It was purple —and ugly.

"Big words," King said. "I smashed it on my last assignment."

"We just learned this in biology class last week. That's why I know the name."

"Okay, and the reason it matters?"

"The man in the video, the one with your face? He didn't have this on his right thumb. I could see his hand plain as day when he shut the trunk. That's how I know you're telling the truth, and I owe you a thank-you."

King was seriously impressed. He hadn't noticed this

detail when he watched the video, but he was also not looking to prove it wasn't him, because he obviously knew it was not. He hadn't even thought about his thumb. But it was ugly enough that it could easily be seen.

"Impressive. And don't thank me yet. I still have to get you out of here alive."

King watched Brittany's demeanor change as she moved her eyes to the window. He hadn't meant to cast doubt on whether he could do that for her, but the way it came out sounded like he might not be too confident.

Before he could explain, she looked back at him and asked,

"But you're, like, really good at this sort of thing, right?"

Now was not the time to be modest. He wasn't great with feelings, but he could tell she needed some reassurance. "I've saved a lot of people under worse conditions. Including the President of the United States."

King watched her breathe a sigh of relief. He reached inside the bag, opened the phone's packaging, and powered it on. "Here, call your dad. Tell him you're okay, and tell him to talk to the director of the CIA and get us some help instead of trying to run me down."

Maybe Brittany had believed him before, and maybe she hadn't, about whether or not King was going to keep her safe. But after seeing the physical discrepancy on the kidnapping video, and now King telling her to call her dad, by the look of elation on her face, he knew he had won her over for good. However, just before King handed her the phone so she could get started on clearing his name, the driver-side door bent inward under the impact of a bone-jarring crash.

11

The impact of the vehicle crashing into his door pushed King's car several feet to the right. Before the car settled, he'd already grabbed Brittany by her tank top and pulled her down behind him onto the floorboard in the backseat.

"Keep your head down and don't move until I come back for you!"

As he shouted to Brittany, his hand searched the floor for his Glock, but it must have been pushed under the seat upon impact. Before he could find it, the barrel of a pistol tapped against his window.

"Hands where I can see them," a man said. He was American, judging by the absence of a Mexican accent.

King slowly raised his hands as he looked up. The glare of the sun on the window didn't allow him to see the man's face, but he certainly couldn't miss the massive size of the man's frame. King knew he only had one shot at surviving, and it wasn't by giving himself up. As he raised his left hand, he ducked as he whipped his hand at the door handle, popping it open, and pushing the door outward as hard as he could. If he hadn't ducked, the bullet would have killed him.

The blast of the gunshot rang out, as did Brittany's scream from the floor of the backseat. King's push of the door only managed to move the end of the gun, not the man holding it. King dove, wrapped his left arm around the man's right leg, and pulled as hard as he could while pushing off the seat of the car. The force of his shoulder into the man's waist and the simultaneous pull on the man's leg should have been enough to knock him backward off his feet. But this man was more like an oak tree, and King's efforts had merely been enough to make him stagger backward.

King pivoted out of his first failed move by spinning on the blacktop to his back. When he looked up, the man towering over him was moving his gun down in King's direction. King whipped his right leg up and managed to clip the man's hand, sending the gun clattering across the parking lot. He swiveled around to face him, then mule-kicked the man in the thighs, which gave him the momentum he needed to do a back roll so he could pop up to his feet.

The foe regaining his balance about six feet from King was a hulking man. His white button-down shirt was tight over large muscles, and the rolled-up sleeves revealed bulging forearms. At six feet three and 220 pounds, King wasn't a small man by any measure, but this guy made him seem it. His buzzed dark hair gave King a military vibe, but his gray dress slacks and black dress shoes said otherwise.

As soon as King rose to his feet, the man in front of him took a fighting stance. Before King could ask any questions about whether this man was CIA or if they were on the same team, the man rushed him. And he was much faster than his size should have allowed. King blocked a hammering overhand right, then ducked under a sweeping left hook. King countered with a right hook to the kidney that elicited only a minor grunt. It should have hurt a lot more. And hitting the man felt more like hitting a brick wall than human flesh.

The man pushed King back with both hands. King's momentum put his back up against a nearby minivan. The man rushed forward and threw another right, but this time it was an elbow. King managed to spin to the side at the last second, and the man's elbow plunged into the minivan's rear window. The man had calculated that he should throw the elbow to mitigate the damage to his hand in case he missed and hit the van. So now King knew the man was strong, fast, tough, and smart. King's only choice was to get dirty.

As the man removed his elbow from inside the van, King whipped a leg kick that struck just above the knee. Solid as a rock. The man ate the kick and finally connected a right hand to the side of King's head, just above the temple. Any lower and he would have been unconscious, because he was seeing stars as he staggered back. King wasn't sure he'd ever been hit that hard. And the bull of a man just kept coming. King blocked the next right with a forearm, parried a left jab, then ducked another right as he changed levels and shot for the man's waist. King didn't want to feel that power again, so he decided to change his advantage by taking the fight to the ground.

However, when King wrapped both arms around the man's waist and pushed forward, the man sprawled his legs back and stopped King from taking him down. He pushed

King's shoulders down to the ground and stepped back. King managed to roll over and avoid the soccer kick that was meant for his head. King bounced up and finally found his voice.

"We're both American, why are you fighting me?" King said.

The man didn't feel like talking. Instead he rushed forward, but King was fast enough to slip sideways at the last second. He watched as the man flew by but stood his ground instead of advancing—hoping to show good faith that he didn't want a fight with a possible friendly.

"Why are you chasing me?" King said with a heaving breath. "I didn't do what they're saying I did."

The man turned to face him. "Yet you have the girl in your car."

He advanced again. King threw up a front push-kick to keep him back. "She's not my hostage. I'm trying to keep her safe."

"That why you stuffed her in the trunk of your car? Why your passport was used in Orange County two days ago, which so happened to be the day she went missing? I don't believe in coincidences, Mr. King. Even if you have served our country. Now hand her over, or—"

This time it was King who became the aggressor. Knowing that the man's next line was going to be something to the effect he would hurt him, King stepped in with a Thai kick to the leg, a left hook to the torso, and a straight right, which the man narrowly avoided by moving his head. King was counting on retaliation, and when the man's forward movement came, King dropped down, wrapped his arms around the man's waist as he wrapped his right leg around the leg in front of him. King pulled with his leg and pushed forward with his upper body. It was a classic Jiu Jitsu take-down, which King rarely didn't finish. This was one of those rare times. The man lifted King up by grabbing under his arms and shrugged him off like a flea. It might be the strongest grip King had ever encountered.

As King took a few steps back to regain balance, he spoke once again, trying to deescalate the situation. "You CIA? Or just a private hire by Senator McKinley? Either way, you're fighting an ally."

It was no use. The man was locked in on a fight. "I know what it's like to have your daughter taken by someone you think is an ally."

He moved toward King again. King's only way out was to fight. He shot his arms up to cover his face as the first strike came. The thud against his defense was powerful. The second punch came, and King jumped back to avoid it, then swung an elbow that pounded against the big man's defense, but it was enough to slow him. As King opened up to throw again, he saw an uppercut coming for his chin. It was thrown with such speed that King didn't see it until it was too late. Purple stars exploded in his vision and the smacking sound of crunching teeth and bare knuckle on chin echoed in his rattled brain.

King stumbled back, trying desperately to settle his declining equilibrium. But he couldn't. He felt a hammering blow pound into his left side, then another shot to the side of his head. Before he could unscramble his brain, his feet were above his head, and he collapsed to the ground on his back. The man didn't stop coming. He jumped on top of King, and it was only King's instincts and ground training that saved him. His body went into autopilot while his mind was still returning from the stratosphere. His legs curled around the man's back, his arms wrapped around the man's neck, and he was holding on for dear life as his wits slowly returned.

Holding the man down by the neck helped keep him from rising up and firing punches down on King. But King had been weakened, and the man was too strong. In an instant King was being lifted off the ground, the large man carrying him as if King weighed half what he did. The man went to slam King back on the blacktop when King let go of his grip and pushed himself off. The move had saved his life.

For the moment.

And only for the briefest moment, because the man was charging right at him. Again.

12

The man running at King was going to kill him. King knew this the moment he saw the look in his eye when the man spoke about his own daughter being taken. King knew this was a fight to the death, and if he didn't catch up, he'd be the one they would bury.

It was time to fight fire with fire.

Rather than retreat, or sidestep, King timed a hard right hand with the man's arrival. The man moved his head, and the punch landed on his shoulder. The miss didn't deter King, he followed it with a left hook, then a right uppercut, then another left hook. None of the punches landed flush, but it had stopped the man's momentum.

King followed the barrage with a knee to the midsection, but it, too, was blocked. Then a left elbow to the man's forearm that was blocking his head, then a right low-kick that landed to the man's right knee. Finally, the man buckled. King capitalized with a left hook to the side of the man's head. He staggered right as King's fist bounced off his temple. King reached behind him and threw an overhand right so hard his shoulder popped out of place on the path forward, but his fist still connected. Pain rifled through every part of his upper body. It was excruciating.

As the man staggered back, a trickle of blood started down from a cut in his forehead––proving the man was human. King's right arm dangled from his shoulder, so he moved in and threw a combo of left hook, right kick, and left uppercut. The man grunted and blood spewed from his mouth when King connected with his chin. King's shoulder was screaming in pain, but he had no time for that. He moved forward and pushed the man back against a black sedan. But before he could twist his hips for another left hook, the man used the car behind him to bounce his momentum forward and clotheslined King at the chest. King spun as he whipped backward and landed hard on his right shoulder.

The good news was his shoulder had inadvertently popped back into place on impact. The bad news was the bear of a man was already on top of him again. His weight was pressed fully on King's body, and his forearm was choking King. King gasped for air but none came. He struggled against the man's strength but couldn't budge him. King tried through punches, but he had zero leverage to get any power behind them. And when his attempts at using Jiu Jitsu to escape via shrimping his legs back and changing the angle failed, the black began to close in.

King could hear some traffic out on the street. When he closed his eyes, for whatever reason he could see his home in Kentucky. All of his friends were there. He could feel himself giving in to the pull of unconsciousness that would finally offer relief from his pain. But then he saw something that ignited a spark deep inside his gut. In the flicker of an old film reel, King saw some of the horrible things he'd endured in his life, having never given up. He saw his mother being gunned down in front of him. The hell of SEAL training flashed by. The first time he'd watched one of his own die in combat. He could see himself holding Sam in his arms—carrying her to safety—after the awful things Sanharib Khatib had done to her in Syria. He saw his father through the window of the door in the basement of Vitalii Dragov's mansion—proof that his father had been the one to betray him.

When King's eyes blinked open, all he saw were the eyes of a fiercely determined man. There was still no air to be found. His eyes shut once again.

He then saw his beloved racehorse, King's Ransom, lying headless in the stall of his barn. The fear on Natalie Rockwell's face when he first saw her rigged to the death machine on the boat in London. His mind then whirled to being at the top of the Ferris wheel in Santa Monica, holding onto the young girl by her fingertips. At the airport in Washington, DC, when the nanobots had just injected Sam and Kyle with the lethal nano chips and he nearly lost two more of the most important people in his life. The reel turned to finding Agent John Karn dead on the couch in Bruges, Belgium. He'd only been there to help King.

It the end, the theme of his final movie changed its tone. King was back at home in his backyard. The sun was high in the sky and shone warmly on his skin. He looked down to his left, and his hand was holding the hand of his blonde-haired, blue-eyed, six-year-old niece. They were walking toward an intimately familiar woman, but the glint of the sun hid her identity. She was holding a baby. His baby. And it was unmistakably so. King began to feel light as over fifteen years of burden began to lift. For the first time in a long time, he was happy. Genuinely so. There was no longer the burden of secrecy, he was no longer a shadow deprived of light, he was alive. And he wanted to see who that woman was—longed to feel her touch. He wanted to hold his child. He wanted to live the movie playing in his mind; even if it wasn't a possibility, he wanted to fight for it. He wasn't ready to leave the ones he loved, present or future.

King's eyes shot open. The determined man was still there—unrelenting. But King no longer wanted to escape the pain he was in; he wanted to embrace it. The feeling of life his mind's eye had showed him after all the despair he'd survived gave him hope. And at the moment, there was only one thing keeping him from getting back the life he hadn't realized his subconscious had so been longing for.

The man's face staring at him changed. There was now a hint of surprise. King's right arm inched down along his side as his lungs continued to fight for air. Near the end of consciousness, right on the brink of shutting down, he conjured every last ounce of life he had left and reached up for the man's groin.

Then he squeezed.

At first there was no change. In King's state of near death, for a moment he thought maybe his mind was playing tricks on him and he'd grabbed the wrong part of the man's body. But as he gave the last of himself to continue the squeeze, there was finally the first sign of movement from the man's forearm.

And the first sign of air.

King inhaled as though he'd been underwater for minutes too long. The oxygen breathed life into his blood, and his blood pumped energy into his muscles. King righted his grip on the man's groin, and more air came his way. The man was forced to lift his arm from King's throat, and when he did, King bucked his hips toward the sky and pushed with the arm still attached to the man's most sensitive area.

King managed to gain top position, and as the man reached down to free his groin from the excruciating pain, King came over the top with an elbow that landed so hard to the man's forehead that the back of his skull bounced off the pavement below. His eyes rolled back in his head, but King, unrelenting himself now, threw another elbow, landing in the same place. This one woke the man back up. Unbelievably, the man was able to get his arms up to his face to block the third elbow, but that didn't stop King from throwing a fourth, then a fifth. When neither of those landed, King began blasting his fists into the ribs of the man. When that forced one of his arms to move downward to block those punches, King came over the top once more and landed a hooking right hand to the man's face, his cheekbone splitting open on contact.

The man had no choice but to flip over onto his stomach to keep from taking more damage. This was every fighter's instinct at the end. It was also the worst thing the man could have done. King forced his arm across the neck of the man below him; then he locked a choke in tight by hooking it with his other arm. When the man felt the power of King's squeeze wrapping around him like a boa constrictor, he rolled back over. This allowed King to cinch the choke by wrapping his legs around the man's hips, thus giving King control of the man's body.

It was over.

The man would never survive King's grip. He desperately rolled a couple of times, flailed about with desperate punches, but it didn't matter; King just rolled with him. King ended up on his back, squeezing the life out of the man who'd almost killed him, and that's when he looked up and saw the back door of the car he'd stolen pop open. Brittany emerged from the car and looked around until she found the two of them on the ground. King watched as her face morphed from scared to confused. She took a step toward King.

"Get back in the car!" King shouted as he gave all his might to ending the man's life in his grasp.

Instead, Brittany squinted her eyes as if she were trying to determine who King held in his arms. Her face changed once more, this time to shock.

"Mister—Mister Raines?"

King looked down at the top of the man's head he was holding. Then back to Brittany. "Get back in the car!"

She took another step forward. "Lawson Raines? What —what are you doing here? Let him go!"

Now it was King who was shocked. "You know him?"

"Yes!" she screamed. "Let him go!"

King released his hold on the man Brittany called Lawson Raines. The man sucked in air as he sat up. Before King could shout to Brittany—who'd just begun walking toward the two of them—to stay back, a mist of red exploded from the side of her head. Her body collapsed to the ground.

Brittany had been shot.

The senator's daughter was dead.

13

"NO! Brittany!"

Lawson Raines shouted as he jumped to his feet.

"Stay down!" King shouted at his back.

But he didn't. The big man was moving quickly across the parking lot. King rose and hit a dead sprint in just two steps. He dove at Lawson's back and tackled him to the ground. The second shot from the sniper rifle crashed through the windshield of the car beside him, which was now providing them cover. Lawson glanced up at the shattered window and realized that would have been his head.

"This is about to get worse," King said. "We have to go!"

"I'm not leaving her!"

King scanned the parking lot. He noticed Lawson's pistol lying on the ground a few feet from him. They were on the ground about four parking spaces over from the car Lawson had rammed King's car with. King looked back over at Lawson.

"I'm not leaving here without her body," Lawson said.

King could see in his eyes there was no talking him out of it. Clearly Lawson knew Brittany personally, so King understood. Before King could respond, two sets of screeching tires filled the quiet around them.

"Get her. Get to the car. And be ready to drive," King said.

Lawson gave him a nod.

"Go now!"

As the words left King's mouth, he sprang to his left, dove across the asphalt, taking Lawson's Sig Sauer in his hand. He rolled onto his back and began firing the moment he saw the first of the gunmen aiming at him from the cars at the parking lot's entrance. Out of the corner of his eye he watched Lawson move toward the fallen girl. He put three bullets in the man aiming at him from the driver's side, then rolled to his feet as he fired three more times at the passenger side. As the men from the second car began to shoot, King dove behind a truck on the row opposite Lawson's vehicle. This would make it harder for him to make it to the car, but averting the gunman's attention to himself would give Lawson time to get Brittany and be ready to drive.

He popped up to his feet and fired straight through the van's windows in the direction of the two remaining gunmen. His objective with the shots was distraction, not actually hitting the men. He was also concerned about the sniper. He heard the report of one more shot, but it didn't hit him, and Lawson was already putting Brittany in the backseat of the car. King wasn't sure, but the line of sight for the sniper to Lawson's car looked to be obstructed by a van. King could only hope this was the case.

King popped back up and shot the man at the passenger

door with his last three rounds. He glanced to Lawson as the magazine clicked empty. Lawson had just entered the car without signal. It occurred to King there was a good chance this Lawson Raines could just leave him there. After all, the two of them did just try to kill each other. King ducked as soon as the magazine was empty, and return fire came from the last remaining gunman. Just as he ducked, a hole bored into the fiberglass of the truck he was taking cover behind, right where he had been standing.

The sniper had turned the weapon on King.

Gunshots were pelting the other side of the truck from the man's semiautomatic rifle at the car. The sniper rifle was trained on King from somewhere in the opposite direction. And there he was without a weapon. There was only open parking lot between him and Lawson in the car. No way he would make it there without getting hit by someone's bullet. He leaned out quickly to peek around the rear bumper. Lawson's car hadn't moved. As soon as he drew back, another sniper round careened off the truck. He reached up and tried the door, but it was locked. Same with the small sedan behind him. He was stuck.

Across the parking lot King heard an engine rev, then tires squealing across pavement. King dropped to his stomach to get a look without being open to the sniper's shot, and he watched as the bottom of Lawson's car was moving in reverse. He was leaving him. King was going to have to find a way out of there by himself.

Then Lawson's car did a 180-degree turn while still in reverse. It was now moving fast toward the front end of the car where a gunman was last shooting. Smoke was rolling from the pavement beneath it. Lawson wasn't leaving; he was taking away one of King's obstacles.

King tucked the Sig Sauer in the back of his belt line and moved to the edge of the front of the truck. The gunman moved his weapon toward Lawson's car right upon impact. The back end of the Audi sedan Lawson was driving slammed into the gunman's car before he could move, and the open door knocked him backward. King stayed in a crouch and ran behind the row of cars between himself and Lawson. That side of the cars also offered cover from the sniper. Just as King rounded the final vehicle, Lawson's car shifted direction and surged forward. The thought that he was leaving once again entered King's mind, but it didn't stay there for long because he watched Lawson's trunk pop open.

As he watched Lawson pull forward, his go bag came to mind. A lot computed at once. Brittany dying would most likely be blamed on him, so the hunt from the United States would only get more intense. From the looks of the men who'd just attacked them from the cars, Raúl Ortega was also trying to run him down. He assumed Brittany also somehow that had something to do with that. Then there was the sniper. Who the hell was he, and even more disturbing, who the hell was he working for? Couldn't be the US—Brittany wouldn't have been the target. And he ruled out Ortega and his cartel because a sniper didn't fit the mold. That meant there were at least three different factions King knew of that were hunting him. So leaving without the go bag was just not an option.

King bolted out from behind the parked cars and sprinted for his stolen car. He signaled Lawson by pointing to the road just beyond the parking lot, but he had no idea if Lawson had seen him. King could almost feel the sights on the sniper rifle honing in on him. It gave him a little extra push in his legs as he pumped his arms running. Before he felt the sting of a bullet or saw the darkness of death, King dove forward behind the side of his car. He tore open the wrecked door, slithered inside, scooped up the Glock on the floorboard, gathered up the bag and pushed across the center console to the passenger seat on his stomach. A bullet crashed through the back windshield and thumped into the dashboard right beside him. He stayed low as he peeked out the window. Lawson's tires squealed as he jerked the car to the left and exited the parking lot.

He had seen King's signal.

King threw the bag onto his back. Another round penetrated the side of the car. The shooter was getting desperate. King pushed the door open and bolted out into the parking lot. He jumped, slid across the hood of a sedan on his ass, and hit the ground running on the other side. Gunshots peppered at his back. It must have been the man from the car Lawson had slammed into. King had no choice but to push forward.

Out of the corner of his eye he could see Lawson's car coming. He kicked into another gear as he ran beside a vehicle in the last row of the parking lot. Another sniper round hit the hood of the car nearest King, just beside his head. Then he was out in the middle of the street. He dodged a moving car in the first lane as Lawson's car moved past him, slowing just enough at King's approach. King put everything he had into his dive, which sent him crashing into the back of the empty trunk. He braced himself as the car accelerated. He rolled over to grab the trunk to pull it shut but before he could, he saw two more cars speeding toward him.

The fight wasn't over. As he slammed the trunk down, plunging himself into darkness, he understood the fight was only just beginning. But at least he was alive to have a fighting chance.

14

S am stood tapping her foot anxiously as she stared out Director Lucas's office window. The landscape in front of her was a patch of trees that led to the Potomac River. Despite the view, the only thing she actually saw was Alexander King in trouble—and no way for her to help him. It wasn't something she was used to, and frankly, it wasn't something she was going to stand for. She'd weighed the options in front of her: stay under Director Lucas's thumb and face no recourse or punishment while King was fighting for his life, or find a way out of Langley and possibly face years in prison, while possibly helping her best friend and partner survive.

It didn't take a lot of thought. Sam walked over to the director's desk and gave it a once-over. She didn't see a phone she could take with her. Instead, she found something better: a set of car keys. She was about to commit treason in the eyes of the CIA, so a little grand theft auto seemed a small pine on a mountain of trees. She turned back toward the door where the two agents were outside standing guard. She went over, opened the door, and walked out like they weren't even there.

"Ma'am?" one of the guards called out to her.

She just kept walking.

He called a little more forceful this time. "Ma'am, you can't leave here."

She turned to face them as they were stalking toward her. "Am I under arrest?"

The two men stopped, looked at each other, then back to her. The large one on the right said, "No ma'am, but we're just following orders. You know how it is."

Before she could protest, she heard screaming coming from the direction of the break room down the hall where she'd left the senator and Director Lucas a while ago. The two agents rushed past her. This was her chance to make her exit without being questioned, but curiosity got the better of her. She was afraid it had to do with Xander, so she couldn't leave without a look.

Sam jogged toward the break room and glanced around the doorway. First her eyes were drawn to the senator who was on his knees, his face buried in his hands, wailing as he sobbed uncontrollably. Sam looked up to what everyone else in the room was focused on—the television. It was immediately clear why the senator was so upset. He had just witnessed his daughter being murdered on national TV.

Sam tuned her ears to what the broadcaster was saying:

We are sorry for the violent nature of the video clip you are watching. It was sent to us just moments ago. This . . . this is Senator Terry McKinley's daughter, being shot in the streets of Mexico City sometime this afternoon. We'll get you more information as soon as we have it.

Sam watched as a large man dragged the girl's body over to a car. The video was taken from a high vantage point with what looked to be a great deal of zoom. The face of the man who was dragging the senator's daughter was hidden by her lifeless body. But Sam could tell by the size of him that it definitely was not Alexander King.

Her stomach dropped.

Where was Xander?

The news anchor continued:

The identity of the man who killed her and dragged her body away has yet to be authenticated, but one must assume it was her alleged kidnapper, former Navy SEAL, Alexander King.

Sam couldn't believe her ears. Someone, somewhere was pointing all of this toward King. They were orchestrating an entire mission of lies against him, mounting visual evidence as they went. Sam could no longer sit idle. They were attacking Xander, and she wasn't going to sit around and wait to see if he could get out of it himself. Some unknown enemy was tipping the scales in their own favor, making King look like a monster. Sam was about to put some weight back on his side of the scale.

While everyone in the building seemed distracted, Sam moved for the elevator. She made it down to the lobby without being seen. She then hurried outside to find Director Lucas's vehicle. She pulled his keys from her pocket and began hitting the lock button. She just followed the beep each time she would hit the button until she found his black Chevy Tahoe. She climbed in and started down the private road. Her last obstacle was the gate, complete with armed guards.

Sam did a quick search, but there was no phone. Her mind was racing. She had no idea who the man was who had lugged Brittany McKinley's body across that parking lot, but worse than that, she had no idea if he'd already killed Alexander King. The gate came into view. She knew it wouldn't be long before Director Lucas found she was missing, subsequently that his car was as well. She also knew his truck had tracking, so she wouldn't get far in it, but she really only needed to make it far enough to find another vehicle.

Luckily, the gate guard waved her through. There hadn't been enough time for anyone to relay down to the gate to stop her from leaving. The commotion in the break room had been large enough to give her room to breathe. But it wouldn't last long. She needed a new car, a new phone, and some information on what the hell was really going on in Mexico City.

15

As the car jerked back and forth, King fumbled for the pulley to push in the backseat from the trunk, but there wasn't one. Instead, his hand finally found a plastic button on the cloth back. When he pressed it, he was able to fold the chair inward. He crawled through to angry shouts from the driver's seat.

"You killed her! It's your fault she's dead!" Lawson shouted as he swerved right onto a different street.

King pushed through and was then thrown into the floor as he tried to avoid touching Brittany's body that was lying in the backseat.

"Don't come up here. I'll kill you while I'm driving."

King pulled himself to a seated position on the floorboard. "Bullshit. Drop the outrage. You would never have opened the trunk for me if you thought I was responsible."

"Who the hell are these guys chasing us?" Lawson changed the subject.

"Raúl Ortega's men."

"Who?"

That told King all he needed to know about whether this man was CIA or not. He would know the name if he was.

"Cartel," King said. "Who the hell are you?"

King crawled across the console to the front seat. Along the way, his go bag brushed Lawson, and Lawson shoved him against the passenger door.

"Keep pushing me and the two cars full of gunmen behind us will be the least of your worries."

"Oh, you mean like back in the parking lot when I whipped your ass?" Lawson said, swerving once again.

King checked his rearview, and the two cars were still on their tail.

"Don't forget what position you were in when I let go of you, Lawson Raines."

Lawson glared over at King. King didn't look away.

"Look, we're on the same team. Can we drop this bull-shit attitude?" King said.

"Same team?" Lawson raised his voice. "I am not and will never be on the same team as someone who kidnaps an innocent girl."

"I didn't kidnap the girl."

"I saw the video. It was pretty conclusive."

"You believe everything you see on the news?"

The two of them were quiet for a moment. King laid his Glock in his lap, took Lawson's pistol he'd picked up off the ground for him earlier from his belt line and laid it on the dash before pulling the go bag from his back. He fished out one of the burner phones and powered it on.

"Look," King said. "I'm CIA. I was set up. I would have never hurt Brittany."

"Yeah, then why is she dead? Huh? That's on you!"

King's frustration boiled over. "Still want to place blame? How 'bout finding a mirror. Brittany was fine in my care until you slammed into my car and started a fight. That sniper would never have had the opportunity to shoot her if it wasn't for you. If it's on anyone, it's on you!"

Lawson took his right hand off the steering wheel and started punching King in the face. King grabbed Lawson's arm and trapped it. Lawson began steering with his knee and punching with his left hand. King just kept blocking.

"Stop! If we both die, we can't find who's really behind this!"

Lawson kept trying to fight.

"Stop fighting me and drive! It's not our fault she's dead. It's whoever set me up that's behind this."

Lawson tore away from King's grip just in time to swerve around a car right in front of them.

"Calm down or we aren't going to survive this," King said.

Lawson pounded the steering wheel with his hand. "She was a good kid. Great kid!" He pounded the steering wheel again.

King grabbed the dash in front of him while Lawson drove wildly down the road.

"I told you who I am," King said calmly. "Now who are you, and why are you here?"

Lawson glared over for a moment; then his face softened. "Brittany is . . . *was* my daughter's babysitter. When she was kidnapped, her father called me to help."

"Why? Who are you?"

"Private investigator now, but was FBI in a different life."

Lawson found an on-ramp to the freeway and kept speeding straight ahead.

King began to dial Dbie's number. "Where'd you learn to fight like that?"

Lawson looked over at King, dead serious. "Prison."

King didn't look shocked. "Let me guess, you were innocent?"

Lawson looked back at the road. "Let me guess, it wasn't you who used your passport at the John Wayne Airport, and it wasn't you in that video."

"Touché," King said. They had finally found some common ground. If Lawson knew what it was like to be set up, it would be easier to realize King was actually an ally. "Look, we aren't going to get away from Ortega and his men. They own this city. Sorry to tell you, you really stepped into it by coming here."

"Then what do you suggest?"

"We're going to have to take the guys behind us out then, ditch the car. We can't take her with us."

"I'm not leaving her behind," Lawson snapped.

"We don't have a choice. Until we can either leave the country or take out Ortega, we will be fighting for our lives. That's not even to mention the sniper and whoever the hell he or she works for."

"I'm not lea—"

"I heard you. But there's no other option. We can hide the car, then I'll have my contact let the embassy know where her body is. They'll pick her up within an hour."

Lawson shot him a look, then turned to the rearview mirror. "You fight well, but do you have any other training?"

"I have all the other training." King hit the call button on the burner phone, then put it on speaker. "But you already knew that, Mister Private Investigator."

"X, you're all right!" Dbie answered.

"I'm not sure that's how I'd describe it, but I'm alive."

"What the hell happened? Who was that man who killed the senator's daughter?"

King looked up at Lawson. It was odd to see such a big man wearing such a worried look.

"What do you mean?" King said.

"The video. It's awful. The whole world watched her get gunned down, then you can see some big guy pulling her into his car. Are you tracking him?"

"He's driving the car I'm in. It wasn't him. How the hell is there another video already?"

"I don't know. It's shot from an angle. Maybe a camera on a building?"

"Dbie, you and I both know if it was security camera footage, it wouldn't have already made news. It had to have been leaked."

"The sniper," Lawson said.

King was thinking the same thing.

"So what are they saying?" King said.

"Well, you can't see the man's face in the video. They're saying it's you, that the police had you surrounded, so you killed her. But I could tell by the man's size that it wasn't you. And why, if you killed her, would you take the time to take her body? It makes no sense."

"Yeah, but as you know, it doesn't have to." King let out a deep breath. "Civilians will believe it either way. Question is, will the CIA?"

"I can't get ahold of Sam. They must be holding her until they find you."

"Shit."

"What can I do?"

"Any IDs on the two Mexican men at the bar the night Brittany was taken?"

"Couple of small-time criminals," Dbie said. "No known connection to Ortega."

Lawson chimed in. "What about the white man the girls were talking to at the bar?"

"X?" Dbie said.

"It's okay, go ahead."

"Former Navy SEAL, Scott Smith. That's all I could find. Well, there are other documents, but they are classified."

"Classified? No discharge papers?"

"Nothing. No record of anything after four years ago. Not even a driver's license."

"Then how the hell did you find him?" King said.

"How do you infiltrate a terrorist camp and take out the leader?" Dbie said. "Some things are too complicated to explain."

"See if you can get more on him. Probably nothing, but no other info on him seems weird."

"On it. Also, I've had no luck with the airport security system yet, so I don't have any leads on who used your passport yet."

"I need to know this," King said.

"Doing all I can. And before you ask, still no word from Zhanna."

"Damnit. Okay. Find Sam, Dbie. Lawson and I are in some deep shit here."

"My hands are tied till she contacts me."

"Once she sees the latest video, she will find a way."

"I thought the same thing," Dbie said. "I'll email all I've found on Raúl Ortega. It's pretty standard drug lord stuff but maybe something will help."

"Any known addresses other than the place downtown?"

"Several."

"Of course," King said. "Nothing is easy."

"Wouldn't be worth doing if it was. I'm going to get back to it. I'll call you when I know something else."

"Thanks, Dbie."

King ended the call. Before he put the phone away, he texted Dbie: *I need all there is to know on Lawson Raines, a PI in Orange County, California.*

"I'll call my partner," Lawson said. "She can help. Investigating is what we do."

"Leave your partner out of it," King told him while he put away his phone and checked the magazine in his Glock. "Trust me, the more people we involve, the more people we put in danger."

"I wasn't asking." Lawson pulled his cell phone from his pocket.

"Oh, good, you still have your easily trackable cell phone on you," King said.

"Don't be a wiseass. It's a burner. You aren't the only one with experience. You actually remind me of Cassie. She thinks she's funny too."

"Oh, you're one of those who thinks to get things done you ... must ... be ... serious ... all ... the ... time. You and my partner, Sam, together would just light up a party."

"Why do you think these guys are hanging back?" Lawson changed the subject. "And not trying to run us off the road?"

"They know there is nowhere for us to go."

"Then let's get rid of them, get Brittany into good hands, then ditch the car. Somebody has to pay for what they did to her."

King pulled and released the slide on his Glock. "I'm glad we're finally on the same page."

16

_____

Lawson sped off the highway, dodged a few cars, and pulled into the gas station on the right after exiting the off-ramp. King jumped out of the car and moved quickly to his right to hide behind a truck. The two cars tailing them slid around the turn of the off-ramp and came to a skidding halt when they noticed Lawson's car. King used the gas pumps beside him as cover as he circled around to flank them. He looked back through the gap and watched as Lawson held his hands up in the air for Ortega's men to see. Two men exited each car and stood behind their open doors, guns extended in front of them.

King made his last move, sprinting fifteen feet to the back of another car that was closer to the gunmen while their focus was on Lawson.

"We aren't the cops," one of the gunmen shouted in a Mexican accent. "There is no surrender!"

King knew the gunfire was coming next, so he stepped out from behind his vehicle and shot the two men closest to him, then dove back behind the car. Just as he and Lawson planned, when the two other gunmen turned their weapons toward King, Lawson pulled his own gun and fired on them while they were distracted. King sat up and poked his head around the car. Lawson's shots had hit their mark. Across from King a mother dove on top of her two kids to protect them from the gunfire. King stood and showed her that he was putting his gun away.

"Police. Everything is okay!" he shouted to her.

"Let's get the hell out of here," Lawson shouted from across the parking lot.

King rounded the car and watched Lawson carrying Brittany in his arms toward one of the gunmen's cars. He felt sad for her. She seemed like a great girl. That sadness, as it often did when he'd failed to help someone, quickly turned to anger. Anger for the senseless loss, anger for her parents who will grieve for the rest of their lives, and anger against the world constantly surrounding him. The world that most Americans know exists but have no idea how insidious it can be.

As he scanned the area for any more possible trouble, King's rising blood pressure instantly peaked when a car came to a screeching stop right beside them. One man already had his gun extended—he had King dead to rights. Lawson couldn't help because he was busy placing Brittany in another car. King glanced around for options, but there were none. He was halfway between the gas pumps and the car they were taking. No cover within diving distance, and no way he could get his Glock up before the man shot him. He'd lost focus, and it might now cost him his life.

King's lack of hope quickly turned to confusion.

"What's your name?" the Latino man said, with zero

Mexican accent. His face was mostly hidden by the shadow of his hat.

"Thomas . . . Thomas Crown," King said.

"Not your bullshit cover. Your real name. I'm not playing." The man glanced down at his gun.

King was dead either way, so it didn't much matter to him if the man new his true identity. "Alexander King."

"That's what I thought. Get your things and get in."

"I'm not coming with you. You'll have to kill me right here."

"I'm not planning on killing you, Mr. King, but the police will be here in a matter of seconds. And I probably don't need to tell you that they will not be taking you to prison."

King looked over at Lawson. He noticed Lawson reaching for his gun. King made eye contact with him and shook his head. Then he looked back at the man, who was now lowering his gun.

"They're coming with me," King said.

"No, just you, Mr. King. We have a war to fight, and the big guy will just get in the way."

King didn't really know what was going on, but clearly this man—even though he was in a metallic green, lowrider Chevy Impala, himself dressed exactly like the gunmen who King and Lawson had just taken out—was not working for Raúl Ortega. And he didn't really know Lawson Raines either, but the fight he'd just endured with him back in the parking lot told him enough to know that Lawson could more than handle his own.

Lawson tucked his gun away and walked around the

car toward the Impala. "If you're going after the men responsible for killing that girl, and for taking shots at us, I assure you I will not get in your way. I'll be leading the way."

The man looked back at King. "Your call. You're the commanding officer."

That told King all he needed to know. Even though it seemed odd this man could know he was ever any sort of rank, it was clear he was on the same team. "Lawson is good to go. And we're dropping the girl somewhere safe before we get going."

King looked over at Lawson, who nodded in appreciation.

"You're the boss," the man said. "But we'd better hurry no matter what we do."

Sirens echoed in the distance. The police were closing in.

"Lawson, put Brittany in the back. I'll get my bag."

The man pulled the Impala over beside the gunmen's cars. King jogged over to Lawson's Audi and pulled out his go bag. His DNA would be in the car along with Brittany's blood, making it even harder to distance himself from the crime in the eyes of the CIA. But he couldn't worry about that at the moment. He'd caught a break with the apparent undercover agent finding them, seemingly willing to fight alongside him and Lawson. Now he had to capitalize on it. It was his only path to redemption.

"Grab all of their weapons. We're going to need them," the man said to King as he approached.

King hurried around to the dead bodies and did as the Latino man said. He picked up the few guns he saw lying around. The sirens were getting closer. Lawson placed Brittany inside and closed the back door. King jumped in the passenger seat.

"Long time, my friend," the man said.

King looked up from the man's outstretched hand, and now that he'd removed his hat, King recognized the face. King grabbed his hand and gave it a firm shake.

"Holy shit," King said. "José Ramirez? How the hell is this possible?"

José was a ghost from missions past. A few years back, King's clandestine crew, Team Reign, was moving in on cartel leader Javier Romero in Sinaloa, Mexico. After infiltrating Romero's compound, the information trail had run cold. José then revealed himself as the undercover agent whom the Director of the CIA at the time, Mary Hartsfield, had used to gain information to get to Romero. José was instrumental in getting King's team to their target.

"I've been undercover here since the last time we crossed paths in Sinaloa," José said as he wheeled the car left out of the gas station parking lot. "I've worked my way up in Ortega's camp for years. I know everything. The minute he said your name a couple of days ago, I couldn't believe it. I knew immediately my time in Ortega's cartel was through. You saved me from Romero in Sinaloa. Now it's time for me to return the favor."

King didn't know what to say. He still couldn't believe his eyes. José had thinned out a bit, but overall he hadn't changed much. He still had his dark hair pulled back in a ponytail and seemed as fit as a soldier.

"I thought the bad guys from my past were the only people I ever ran into again. Good to see you, José. And thank you." King looked back over his shoulder and nodded to Lawson. Lawson nodded in return. "This is Lawson

Raines. He and I just met, and before he says anything about our initial meeting, just know he hits like a girl."

That was the first smile King had seen on the big man's face. It was good to know there was a sense of humor in there somewhere. Even while evil and chaos surrounded them.

José studied King's face. "Yeah? One hell of a hard-hitting girl by the looks of it."

King pulled down the visor and checked his face. A long trail of dried blood ran down from his swollen right eye.

"LUCKY SHOT," King said.

José laughed. "We need to regroup and be ready to strike while Ortega has a lot of his men out looking for you. Where do you want to take the girl?"

"Closest hospital. I'll have my contact get the embassy to pick up her body."

"Hospital De Jesus is right around the corner."

King opened his burner and dialed Dbie. He was ready to get Brittany in a place where her body could be properly escorted back to her family. After that was done, he would be ready for war.

17

Sam crossed the bridge from Langley over the Potomac River. She didn't know what the town she was driving toward was called, but it didn't matter. Her only goal was to pick up a couple of prepaid phones and ditch Director Lucas's SUV. It was a literal magnet for her to get caught. As soon as Robert found out Sam was gone and had taken his Tahoe, they would track her and be on her in a matter of minutes.

She had punched "drugstore" in the Tahoe's GPS, and a CVS pharmacy came up across the river. It was farther than she wanted to go, but it was at least a place she knew would have phones. She needed to talk to Dbie to make sure King was still checking in, and she had to get ahold of Kyle Hamilton. Kyle was King's best friend from childhood, and they'd been glued at the hip until King was forced to disappear two years ago. Kyle had no idea Xander was still alive, but she knew that, like the rest of the world, he'd probably already seen the news report. She imagined her cell phone, since it had been confiscated, probably had about thirty missed calls from Kyle.

She wasn't sure exactly how she was going to explain. Kyle would obviously be overjoyed that his best friend was still alive, but he would be devastated that he'd been kept in the dark. No matter how much she or King would try to explain it to him, he wouldn't understand. He would undoubtedly wonder why he hadn't been the one to know instead of Sam. And no amount of explaining—that it was part of how King could keep him safe—would ever make it clear.

"Sam?"

Sam jumped when Director Lucas's voice came through the speakers in the Tahoe.

"Turn my SUV around and bring it back to headquarters now, and I'll chalk this up to you just desperately wanting to help a friend."

Sam turned off the bridge. She was only a mile from the CVS. "You know I can't do that, Robert."

"Damnit, Sam. You're leaving me no choice. King is considered a fugitive right now, and until we can prove otherwise, he—"

"Prove otherwise?" Sam interrupted. Her voice near a shout. "Are you joking? Ask the President of the United States of America if Alexander King is a fugitive. Go on. Call him. I'll wait. Because the only reason you can even call him is because Alexander King kept him from dying. Or did that escape your memory?"

"Sam, I—"

"Or why don't you check the headlines from a month ago, would you? Check and see if there is a headline about the deadliest pandemic in world history that wiped out half of all American citizens. Oh, you can't, can you? Because those headlines don't exist, do they, Robert? D'ya mind telling me why those headlines don't exist?"

"Sam, point taken. No one knows more than I do what an asset King and yourself have been to this country. But—"

"No buts! That's it. Just stop right there. You and I both know Xander is not capable of these things. I don't care how it looks in the news or otherwise. So if you won't start treating him as the patriot that he is, I will. I will bring him home safe. Because *that* is what allies do."

Director Lucas started to protest, but Sam hit the voice volume button until she could no longer hear him. She was enraged. All the things Xander had done in his life to protect the country he loves, and one video threatened to wipe it all away. Sam knew that technology was the devil itself. She knew it from the moment she was injected with a deadly chip from a robot the size of a mosquito. But she never thought it might be the thing that would bring their team down. She was determined for it not to be.

Sam pressed the pedal to the floor as she sped toward the pharmacy. She was only about a quarter of a mile away. The Tahoe was steadily gaining speed until all of a sudden the dashboard went blank and the vehicle stopped accelerating. She stomped on the brake pedal, but it wasn't working. Director Lucas had the power remotely shut down; he didn't give a damn about what might happen to her inside. She steered around a car, then pressed her left foot slowly on the emergency brake. Finally, the Tahoe began to slow until she brought it to a stop. She could see the CVS sign just a couple of blocks away. She jumped out of the truck and sprinted toward it. She could hear the sirens blaring in the distance. They were headed her way.

Sam bounded into the pharmacy. She scoured the aisles for the proper section and grabbed three phones with prepaid SIM cards. As she was paying for them at the counter, she saw two police cars go by through the windows of the automatic doors. The checkout clerk followed Sam's eyes to the door, then looked down at the phones.

"You're not running from anyone, are you?" The lady smiled when she said it. It was more of a joke than a real question.

"You have a back door?" Sam asked, not smiling.

The clerk lost her smile. "I don't want any trouble."

"Neither do I. That back door then?"

"Through the employee door on the back wall," she said while pointing.

"Do me a favor, yeah?" Sam grabbed the plastic bag of phones.

"Uh, okay."

"Tell the agents who come in here looking for me in just a moment that they can tell the CIA director that while loyalty can sometimes be difficult, it should always be an easy decision."

Sam only received a blank stare followed by a nod. It was worth a shot. She stepped away and jogged toward the back door.

"I love your accent," the clerk called to her.

Sam was already gone.

18

Apricot rays of a setting sun beamed through the kitchen window in José Ramirez's apartment. He called it his own personal safe house, one that neither Raúl Ortega nor the US government knew about. He'd learned from being trapped in the drug lord's cartel back in Sinaloa that it was smart to keep a back door open for himself. A lesson that was reinforced by the way the CIA was currently turning their back on Alexander King.

After getting in the car with José earlier, they stopped by the hospital and found an empty ambulance. They placed Brittany in the back, and King had Dbie line up someone from the embassy to go pick up her body. Then they went straight to José's place.

"Okay, first, let's lay out everything we know." King walked over and set a cup of coffee on the small, round kitchen table. "I'll start from my angle. Then you guys tell me yours, and hopefully it will give us some answers."

Lawson and José gave him a nod.

"I was down here simply to gather some intel on Raúl

Ortega. Word was that he was expanding from drugs to human trafficking. In hindsight, this was the first red flag for me, because I've never been sent on an intel-only mission."

"Never?" Lawson said. "Isn't that about the only thing you agency guys are supposed to do? Gather intelligence?"

"You were FBI, right?" King said.

Lawson nodded.

"Then you know how much you color outside the lines of the official statements."

"I didn't even have lines," Lawson said. "Part of what my director hated, yet loved, about me."

"Sounds like you guys have a lot in common," José said. "As for me, I always stay inside the lines." He smirked as he glanced around his secret apartment.

"Yeah," King said. "Anyway, last night I was watching Ortega's place downtown when I saw him pushing a girl inside. Which now I'm assuming was Brittany McKinley."

"It was," José confirmed. "I can tell you what I knew—"

"Let me finish first, then you go," King interrupted. "I woke up the next morning, drove Cali to the airport, and while I was extending my car rental, Ortega's men put Brittany in my trunk. They filmed someone doing this and made a fake with my face on the body to frame me. And they did it fast."

"Manuel Cortez is his name," José jumped in. "And he did it right there in the parking lot, almost a half an hour before you made it back to the car. He's Ortega's relation, been grooming him since he was a kid just for things like this. He's a tech genius."

"You were there?" King said.

"I was. And when I saw that you really were there, too, that's when I knew I was finished spying on Ortega."

"Cheers to that," King said.

"Speaking of cheers," Lawson said, raising his coffee cup, "got anything to go with this to make it taste better?"

José got up. "Of course I do." He walked over to a cabinet above the stove and grabbed a bottle of tequila.

Lawson glanced up at King. King met his eyes, and they both shook their heads at the same time. "He's not from where we're from," Lawson said.

"Wait, you're from Kentucky?" King said.

Lawson smiled.

"No shit? How'd you know I was?"

Lawson raised an eyebrow. "Everyone knows you're from Kentucky, rich boy. I watched you on TV when your horse won the Derby."

King sighed as he ran his fingers through his hair. "A different lifetime, I'm afraid."

"Yeah, I know what that's like," Lawson said as he stared off into space. King could tell there was a lot of story there.

"So you want some tequila for your coffee or not?" José was confused.

"What Lawson is trying to say is, you don't have anything brown in that cabinet, do you?"

José held a blank expression.

"Bourbon, José. Bourbon. You know, the most famous thing about Kentucky?" King said.

"Oh, yeah. No, no bourbon. And I thought fried chicken was the most famous thing from Kentucky. It is down here anyway."

King and Lawson both rolled their eyes. Then King remembered the two airplane bottles of bourbon Sam always stashed in his go bag. He walked over, pulled them out, and held them up as he came back to the table.

"Sam always takes care of me," King said as he opened one and poured it into Lawson's mug.

"Remind me to thank him when I see him," Lawson said.

"Her. She's the one who keeps me in line."

"Yeah? I've got someone like that too." Lawson gave his spiked coffee a swirl. "And I need to call her and check in."

King poured bourbon into his coffee and stirred it with his finger. "Can we finish here first?"

"Sure," Lawson said. Then he held up his mug as José finished adding tequila to his coffee. "To José, for scooping us up." Lawson then looked up at King. "And to the gods for not letting us kill each other."

They clinked mugs.

Lawson paused with his mug at his lips. "And to whoever is responsible for Brittany being dead, that we get the chance to give them what they deserve."

The three men sipped their coffee. The last of the toast brought back their focus.

"You guys know the rest after the airport from my end," King said. "José, fill us in."

"Two nights ago was the first time I heard your name mentioned. I wasn't really supposed to, but I am high up enough to have heard it in passing. Needless to say, I did my best to be around to hear what Ortega was saying after that. So, to keep from getting your hopes up, I don't know the who or the why, but I definitely know Ortega was involved with setting you up."

"Isn't that the who in question?" King said.

"Yes, but from what I gather, not entirely," José said. "Everything I heard came through secondhand knowledge. Other guys closer to Ortega. But the gist is that two days ago wasn't the first time your name was brought up by Ortega."

"I have never even been to Mexico City. Why would I be on his radar?"

"Well, I was trying to dig into that without looking suspicious, but if I had to guess, Ortega's move into human trafficking probably had something to do with it."

"Why?" King said. "You think he had some sort of connection to Romero in Sinaloa?"

"Maybe. Or maybe just knowing you were the one who shut Romero down made him want to strike first against you."

"But until this fake video of me surfaced, I didn't exist. Remember?"

José shrugged his shoulders. "X, one of the many differences between Mexico and America is that it isn't that uncommon for someone to 'disappear' here."

"No," Lawson chimed in, "King is right, it made national news when he 'died.' No way Ortega had knowledge of King being alive, especially enough to know to set him up. This has to be coming from someone who has access to the knowledge that you never stopped operating for the CIA."

"Not possible," King said quickly.

Lawson sat up in his seat. "Possible or not, it's the *only* possible explanation."

King let that sink in. He'd been burnt by "allies" before. So it wasn't disbelief that the good guys could betray him that made him so sure it wasn't someone on the inside. It was just the fact that the only people who knew he was alive were people he trusted implicitly. Director Lucas wasn't a traitor. Sam and the people on King's own team would never flip. And that left the President of the United States, and he would never turn on his country. He was a rare man of integrity.

"I hear what you're saying, Lawson," King said. "But I'm a ghost. Anyone who ever wanted me dead are either buried themselves or satisfied I'm gone."

"You sure about that?" Lawson looked him dead in the eye. "Because I was put in jail by people I trusted. For the murder of my wife. I spent ten years rotting there while my daughter grew up without me. So I would take another scroll through your Rolodex of enemies before you're certain it isn't possible."

Lawson was right. That a cartel leader would set King up just didn't make sense. It was as if someone not only wanted King dead but wanted his entire life of service to be forever tarnished along with it.

"This is what I do for a living, King," Lawson said. "And from where I sit, this one is personal. From the looks of it, they don't just care that you're dead; they want to burn your entire life down in the process."

"You're talking about the sniper?" King said.

"Yeah. Why the hell wouldn't they just shoot you? Shooting Brittany further cemented that you'd lost your edge, and maybe your mind. Someone is playing with you. They know your moves before you make them. I found you, so why couldn't they?"

King had thought the same about the sniper. He also wanted to know how Lawson had found him, but first he needed to ask José a question. "So who was it?"

José looked confused when King stared at him. "What?"

"You know Ortega's men. Who was the sniper?"

José shook his head. "That wasn't one of Ortega's men. He could have hired some ex-military man without me knowing, but he would have shot you instead of the girl. Someone may want to tear you down, X, but Ortega is just a middle man. I agree with Lawson. Ortega wouldn't have gone through the trouble of making fake videos if he were the one who wanted you. He would have just shot you dead in the airport parking garage."

"Okay," King said. "So we all agree it's someone else who is after me. Now how am I supposed to find out who? I only have one resource at the moment, and she is as much a secret as I am. So she can't even collaborate with my agency."

Before anyone could respond, King's burner began to ring. He pulled it from his pocket and answered it.

"What the hell is going on?" Dbie's voice was a bit frayed.

"I'm being hunted by a cartel leader and an unknown sniper. What's up with you?"

"No, X. I mean the video."

"The fake? It was shot by Ortega's men in the parking garage. Why?"

"Not that video, Xander. The new video coverage on the news."

King's stomach dropped. "What is it?"

"Turn on the news. You're not going to believe it. It's so ridiculous."

King ended the call. "You have American channels on that TV?" King pointed to the corner of the room.

"No, just on my iPad. Why?"

José reached behind him on the kitchen counter and picked up a tablet.

"Pull up the news," King said.

José opened the iPad and pressed a few buttons, then set it up on its stand so all of them could see.

"Right there, that's you," Lawson pointed.

King's eyes scoured the busy home page of an American news site. Then sure enough, at the bottom right of the page, there was a thumbnail-sized photo of his face. It had a little play symbol in the middle of it. It was a video. José reached over and tapped it. The video filled the screen, and King couldn't believe what he saw. It was his home in Kentucky, with maybe a dozen police cars in the circular driveway at the front of the house. The graphic at the bottom read, "*Rogue Agent's House Raided, Cocaine Everywhere.*" Then the video swiped to a shot of policemen carrying out large black bags from the stables.

"They're trying to bury you for real this time," José said.

Though King's unsure mind was racing—running through all the people who had ever crossed his path and might want to take him down—he was still certain of one thing. Himself.

"Yeah? Well, they picked the wrong guy."

19

As the light behind the cloudy skies began to disappear, Sam stepped out of her cab at Dulles International Airport. It was only a twenty-five-minute drive, so she didn't get a lot of time to figure out exactly what she could do to help Xander's situation. She had tried to call Dbie, but she didn't answer. Then her phone began to ring, and only one person would have the new burner number.

"Dbie, thank God. Have you spoken with X?"

"That's who I was on the phone with when you called. I was hoping it was you. Since this isn't your number, I'm assuming Director Lucas isn't aware you're calling?"

"I snuck away, you could say. Is Xander all right?"

"Well . . . he's in bad shape, even by X's extreme standards, I suppose. Especially after the new video. But he's alive, so that's good."

Sam's pulse quickened as she entered the airport. "New video?"

"Oh yeah, you probably haven't—"

"What is it?"

"They set him up, Sam."

"Yeah, I know he's been set up, but what's the new video?"

"No, I mean that is what the new video is. They're coming at him from all angles."

"Would you just spit it out already?"

"It's a news report. Someone stashed a bunch of kilos of cocaine in the stables in Lexington. They actually took it to his personal home."

Sam couldn't believe her ears. "What?"

"Yeah, cops were carrying out bags of it. Now he looks like he's not only part of some south-of-the-border trafficking ring but part of the cartel as well. With the video of him taking the girl and now this, if I didn't know him, I would for sure believe he was guilty."

"A real voice of positivity, are you?"

"Just being real, Sam. It's bad. And he has no one to help him."

Sam stopped in front of a long row of ticketing counters.

"He will soon. I'm at Dulles in DC. Get me the next flight out to Mexico City under my Beverly Tanner passport and credit card. I have both with me. You still have the info, right?"

"I do. Looking now. How'd you manage to keep Director Lucas from finding your fake passport and credit card?"

"Hid them in my knickers. The moment I knew they were going to keep me from helping Xander, I put them there for safekeeping."

"Good thinking. Okay, go to the United Airlines counter. I just booked you on the 6:35 nonstop to Mexico City. Remember, use your Beverly ID."

"Quick work. Give me Xander's burner number. I'll call him while I race to my plane."

"Will do."

"Talk to you—"

"One other thing," Dbie interrupted. "Kyle has called me no less than forty times since the video ran this morning. I can't keep avoiding him."

"I know. It's time he knew the truth. I'll call him in a moment."

Dbie sighed. "Thank God. I was getting boob sweat just thinking about having that convo with him."

"You're disgusting."

"Thank you."

Sam ended the call and walked up to the United ticket counter. There were no hitches in using her fake identification. She breezed through security and began the walk to her gate. She was good on time and noticed she was feeling a bit hungry. However, each fast food restaurant she passed, she grew more disgusted with her available choices. She would just have wine on the plane for dinner. She needed that drink right then, because she was about to make one man very happy and very angry at the same time.

Dbie's text with Xander's burner number came in, but she closed that out and dialed Kyle's number instead.

"Hello?"

It had been a couple of weeks since she'd spoken with Kyle. It was probably the longest she'd gone since she'd met him several years ago. There was an eagerness in his tone, she could sense it immediately. She knew most all of his little quirks. Partly because she had spent so much time around him and Xander throughout the years of vigilante missions. That and Kyle and Xander were almost literally joined at the hip. The other reason she knew him so well was of course because they had been intimate for a time. Something she didn't regret, but it was clearly a mistake for two close friends, as they had become.

Part of her loved Kyle, and part of him drove her mad. All of that didn't matter now. This was the second most difficult thing she would ever have to tell him. The first being the day she'd told him Alexander King was dead. Now she had to explain why the person closest to Xander wasn't chosen to know he had always been alive.

"It's me," she said.

"Oh, thank God. I've been calling you all day! I'm assuming by the burner number that shit's gone wrong for you since this bullshit of trying to defame a dead man is running all over the news. Why would they do this to Xander? Why can't they just let him rest in peace?"

Sam took a breath.

"Sam?"

"Xander is alive."

Band-Aid approach.

"Sam, I know you've never had the best sense of humor, but even you have to know that isn't funny."

"Kyle, it's not a joke. I'm sorry you weren't privy to know, but he's alive. He had to fake his death to keep us alive two years ago, and he's been running covert missions ever since. Including taking down Saajid and Husaam Hammoud."

Kyle didn't say anything. Sam could hear him breathing heavy into the phone with some crowd noise behind him. He mentioned how much the man in the videos that surfaced from Greece last year had looked like Xander, but he'd never actually suspected what he thought was impossible.

"He did it to keep you safe, Kyle. You should be happy. Xander is—"

"Just be quiet, Sam. Not another word."

Sam was approaching her gate. She made it with fifteen minutes to spare. She was going to let Kyle have all the time he needed. She was just happy he didn't hang up.

"Where are you?" Kyle said.

"DC. Where are you?"

"I just landed here, too, at Dulles airport. I left Toronto as soon as I saw the video and couldn't get ahold of you. I wanted to help take down whoever was smearing X's good name, but turns out I don't even know Xander myself. So what's the point?"

"Kyle, I know you are confused right now, and don't know which way is up, but I need you to get to gate A12 immediately. Like, run."

"No, I'm going back to Toronto and finish my assignment there. To hell with you guys."

Sam scanned her ticket and walked down the jetway. "I know you don't mean that. I'm sorry we tried to protect you, but—"

"Don't!" Kyle shouted. "I am not the man you met when Xander first brought you to the States. I am an agent, too, and a damn good one. I don't need your protection, and I didn't need it two years ago either. What I needed was my best friend not to be dead!"

Sam stepped onto the plane and held her hand over the phone so Kyle couldn't hear her. Then she approached the flight attendant. "Hello. I know you've got to close the door soon, but can you please delay it as long as possible? My brother, whom I haven't seen in years, is trying to make the flight, and I would be so grateful if you could help."

The blonde-haired, blue-eyed attendant smiled and put her hand on Sam's shoulder. "Aw, that's so sweet. I have a brother too." Then she winked. "I'm not sure I can help, but I'll do everything I can."

"Thank you," Sam said. Then she uncovered the phone. "Please, Kyle, let's have this talk face-to-face. Right now. Xander is the most wanted man in the world at the moment, and he's being pinned down by a cartel leader and hunted by the CIA. I know we've hurt you, but he needs us. You know he'd be there for you."

"Would he? Or would he be dead?"

"I'm begging you. Gate A12 to Mexico City. They're about to close the doors."

The line went dead. She knew the call was going to be bad, but that had actually gone worse than she'd expected. She took her seat in the second row of first class. A different flight attendant walked by, and she got his attention.

"Yes, ma'am, how can I help you?"

"Red wine. Doesn't matter the vintage or type."

"Coming right up."

Sam took out her phone, opened the text from Dbie, and pressed the number to call Xander's burner phone. He wouldn't be happy that he wasn't the one who got to tell Kyle himself, but he would be glad Sam was coming to help him. One out of two wasn't bad.

20

K ing, Lawson, and José took inventory of their weapons. All in all they had a decent amount of armory. But it wouldn't be enough if they didn't catch Ortega by surprise. One of Ortega's men had just called José to check in. José explained that he had just missed King at the spot where the girl was killed. They told José that someone had taken the girl to the hospital and the US Embassy found her body. They needed him to search the east side of the city before meeting them at the St. Regis hotel downtown.

While José and Lawson made sure everything was locked and loaded, and José began plotting their course, King slipped away to the restroom. He needed to get his mind right. He shut the door behind him, and when he passed the mirror, it was the first time he noticed the damage done by Lawson's fists. His first thought was that he'd had worse, but really, he wasn't sure he had.

"How do you always get yourself into these messes?" he asked himself.

. . .

HE THOUGHT about how the day started, with him being upset with himself that he'd let Ortega walk the girl into his place and did nothing about it. And after all the crazy in-between that had happened, the girl was shot and killed anyway. For what? That was the question King couldn't answer. None of it made sense to him except if it were some sort of personal vendetta. Otherwise, why take the time to frame King for taking the girl, and for the drugs at his home in Kentucky, if no one knew Ortega had even taken the girl?

There was clearly something deeper going on, but that brought him to why he needed to get away to think. Ortega must have had a hand in setting King up. But was he the only one? King had to think past Ortega. He had to understand for himself if it was even worth it to go after the guy right now. He understood Lawson's motivation. Revenge. Lawson was obviously the type of man who not only didn't back down from fights but ran toward them. King recognized himself in that trait. But that wasn't always the best course of action. Running in undermanned usually only served to put someone in more danger than necessary. If King could prove Ortega killed Brittany, the US would send an army after him. Not just a three-man team who hadn't ever worked together before.

However, what if King couldn't prove Ortega killed Brittany and planted the drugs? Then what? Ortega goes on being the criminal scumbag that he is, and King is still left flapping in the wind with no place to call home. On the run from the government he'd spent his entire adult life protecting.

King turned on the faucet, cupped his hands to fill them

with water, and splashed his face. Going to war with someone as well armored as Raúl Ortega was no small thing. And as with every time he found himself in this sort of situation, all he wanted to do was talk to Sam.

King's burner phone began to ring. He dried his hands and hoped Dbie didn't have another awful thing to tell him as he pulled out his phone.

"I can't take any more bad news, Dbie. So just hang up if that's what you've got."

"Well," a familiar British accent tickled his ear, "don't you sound like Sally Sadsack!"

"Sam!"

"You didn't think I was going to let you have all the fun, now did you?"

"Can you believe this mess?" King stepped to the right and sat on the closed toilet.

"I mean, it is *you*, Xander. So I'm hard-pressed to be surprised. But whomever you've pissed off this time, they are certainly out for your head."

"Unreal, right?"

"Where are you? Are you all right?"

"Remember José Ramirez?" King said. "The undercover agent from Sinaloa?"

"That wasn't the big man pulling the girl into the car in the video, was it?"

"No, but he's with me too. PI hired by Senator McKinley. Long story. Anyway, I'm at José's secret apartment in Mexico City. He's been undercover in Ortega's camp for almost two years."

"Not any longer, I suppose."

"He knows where Ortega is. We're going to hit him while he thinks I'm on the run."

Sam was quiet. King let her take everything in.

"Don't do that yet. I'm on an airplane now. I'll be to you by ten o'clock."

"I knew you'd find a way. You didn't have to kill Director Lucas, did you?" He was sarcastic.

"No," Sam said. "But that doesn't mean I didn't want to."

"Be careful coming in. There are eyes everywhere. I can now account for most of it being Ortega's men, except for one sniper."

"Sniper? The one who shot Brittany McKinley?"

"Yeah, what do you make of it?"

Sam paused. "Certainly not cartel, but that doesn't mean it's one of ours."

"All the enemies we've made across the world, could be from anywhere," King said.

"My point exactly."

King's mind narrowed on one individual in particular who he knew would one day come for him. "You don't think it could be Bentley Martin, do you?"

Bentley was the girl he'd saved from a car bomb back in London. After trying to keep her safe, she murdered Agent John Karn in cold blood and turned out to be a supremely trained terrorist. Her final vow was revenge against King for killing her terrorist-funding father, Andonios Maragos.

"Could be," Sam said. "But not likely. As much as I hate to say it, and even though I just told you it didn't mean the sniper was one of ours, it sure looks like someone with a lot of American connections is trying to bring you down."

"Great, so we still have no idea."

"No. So keep your head down and wait till I arrive. At least we'll be two more numbers with guns."

"*Two* more?" King said.

Sam let out a sigh.

"What is it, Sam? What happened?"

"I told Kyle you are alive."

"What?!" King stood and paced the tiny bathroom in circles. "You know I wanted to be the one to explain things to him!"

"What did you want me to do, Xander? He saw the video. He'd been calling Dbie and myself all day. He left his post in Toronto even though he thought you were still dead. Just to go and kill the people who he thought were tarnishing his closest friend's name."

King was angry, but not at Sam. He was mad at himself. He knew he should have approached Kyle long ago, but he didn't. He was afraid to open his relationship back up to Kyle because he knew he would never see him. King was supposed to be dead, and Kyle had his own assignments. But now he knew it had been a mistake to wait.

"He's pissed, isn't he?" King said. His voice was calm.

"He is. With you, me, and apparently the world."

"Damn, I should have—"

"Xander, I have to go," Sam interrupted. "He just got on the plane. We'll see you in a couple of hours."

King's emotions were swirling. A lot was going on at the same time. But one thing a good operator does about as well as anything is compartmentalize. He started the day compartmentalizing his feelings about Cali leaving—burying them until he knew he could see her again. Now he had to avoid thinking about being reunited with a friend he'd kept a terrible secret from. A painful secret, for his friend. But that had to get buried, too, because he was about to have people's lives in his hands, and you can't be of a split mind when bullets are flying.

Either way, he was glad Sam and Kyle were on their way. They made the chances for success jump dramatically in the good guys' favor. And he couldn't wait to give his old friend a big bear hug. That is, if he would accept it.

21

S am ended the call and stood to greet Kyle. He had just entered the plane, and the stewardess stopped him to ask a question. His short, dark hair was a bit of a mess. His square jaw seemed even more jagged than the last time she'd seen him. He had always been in great shape, but his 6'3" frame now seemed even more lean.

When Kyle caught her eye, his usual elated smile when he saw her was instead a disappointed dip of the head. Sam lowered her outstretched arms and took her seat.

"I'd say nice to see you," Sam said, "but it's clear that sentiment won't be returned."

Kyle placed his messenger bag beneath the seat in front of him, sat back, and let out a deep sigh. He smiled at the stewardess who was bringing him an airplane bottle of bourbon.

"Thank you," Kyle told her. "Don't run off too far, okay?"

The blue-eyed brunette batted her eyebrows and flashed a million-dollar smile. Then she craned her neck all around the plane. "Not too many places to hide. I'm sure you'll find me."

Kyle winked.

The stewardess giggled.

"I see you haven't changed a bit," Sam said, unable to bite her tongue.

"Don't." Kyle sipped his bourbon. "We're not friends right now."

"That's mature. All right then, what are we?"

"Colleagues." His tone was flat. His eyes were watching the United logo animate on the headrest television.

"I understand you're upset, Kyle. You have every right to be. But—"

"No buts necessary," Kyle said, turning toward her. "You can just leave it at I 'have every right to be.' Then just leave me alone."

"Fine. Just want you to know I spoke with X right before you boarded. He's safe . . . for now."

Kyle faced forward again; he didn't comment. It was ten minutes past the designated time to shut the cabin door. Sam thought it was the stewardess helping her out by stalling, but it should have been shut immediately after Kyle boarded. Sam hoped there wasn't any mechanical issues. The last thing she needed was for the plane to be delayed. One reason was she knew the CIA would be watching; the other was Xander couldn't afford her and Kyle arriving late.

As two men in black suits stepped onto the plane, she knew instantly it was the first of her concerns that was going to keep her and Kyle from getting to Xander on time.

"Damn it," Sam said.

Kyle's head swiveled toward her; then he followed her eyes to the front of the plane.

"Did you tell *anyone* you were coming here?" Sam said. "To DC?"

"No. I'm assuming those two are here for us?"

"How did they find me so quickly?"

"So that's a yes?" Kyle said.

Then the two men stepped forward to the second row. The first man with a military-style buzz cut looked straight at Sam as he held out an FBI credential.

"Samantha Harrison?"

"Sorry, you're mistaken. I'm Beverly Tanner. Guess I just have one of those faces."

"Ms. Harrison, you're coming with us."

The man reached forward, but Kyle slapped away his arm. "The lady said her name was Tanner. Move on, fellas."

The man pulled back his sport coat to reveal a pistol tucked inside his shoulder holster. "Okay then, smart guy, *both* of you are coming with us."

Kyle started to rise to his feet in protest, but Sam placed her hand on his arm. Her processor worked fast. She knew Kyle was going to show his CIA credentials to let the men know they had no authority over him, but she also knew it wouldn't matter. Not because they were FBI, but because the pistol in the man's holster was a Beretta. The FBI had been issuing Glocks as their standard pistol since 2016. There was a chance it could be the man's personal sidearm that he carries as a backup, but that nuance coupled with the way his partner's eyes kept jumping all around the plane in a nervous twitch, Sam could feel something was off.

"All right, we'll come along," Sam said.

Kyle's expression turned to shock.

Sam knew if she fought the men on going with them, they wouldn't be afraid to pull their weapons and shoot right there. And while they may not hit Sam or Kyle, someone else would surely be injured or worse, in these tight quarters. Though exiting the plane was the last thing she wanted to do, she knew there was no other option. Either way, she and Kyle weren't leaving on that plane, whether she fought them in the aisle or not. Everyone on the plane would be detained if there was a violent incident.

"Sam, they—"

"They caught us, Kyle. Let's just go and take our medicine."

Kyle's face brightened. He knew Sam would never surrender. She always knew Kyle's processor was a few bits slower than her own. Kyle fell in line, and the two men actually smiled when Sam and Kyle didn't put up a fight. Also not something common of an agent. Sam just hoped these two were the only ones at the airport who had come for them. But she figured that wouldn't be the case. Men like these ran in packs.

Sam reached down for her bag and simultaneously hit the CALL button on her phone as she slid it into her pocket. It would dial the last number she spoke to.

Alexander King.

The two men ushered them out in front, and as Sam walked behind Kyle toward the door, there were two more men waiting in the jetway. Absolutely terrible news. She didn't know who they were or whom they worked for, but she knew they weren't going to be taking them to FBI headquarters, and definitely not back to Langley. The question wasn't *if* she and Kyle were going to have to fight to get away from these men, but when.

Either way, they weren't going to be in Mexico City any time soon.

22

King walked back out into the living area of José's small apartment. José was pointing to something on a map.

"Sorry for the delay," King said. "Had to take a call. You boys get everything worked out?"

José moved his finger on the map. "Here is where Ortega is for the night. He keeps a suite at the St. Regis when he believes his properties could be compromised." He looked up at King. "Since you are still on the loose, he's playing it safe here. He will have maybe four men inside the suite with him. Two in a vehicle in the parking lot watching the front door, and of course a literal army that could be dispatched in minutes."

"So basically it's suicide," Lawson said.

"Let's look at this from another angle," King said. "Lawson, you obviously are only here for revenge. You have no other motivation."

Lawson shrugged.

"José, I'm assuming you just want to finish what you started and bring an end to your long undercover mission."

José nodded. "Basically, yeah."

"And my motivation is to clear my name," King said. Then he held up his hand to Lawson who was about to speak. "I also want to stop Ortega from being able to do this to other girls, Lawson. As José knows, I've laid my life on the line before to stop a human trafficker. My point is, the two of you can just walk away, and should. No one knows you're involved, and it is not worth risking your life for this today. We are too outnumbered, and we don't have any other sort of advantage in the situation that can help us win."

"We know where Ortega is," Lawson said. "That isn't an advantage?"

King looked at José. "Correct me if I'm wrong, but I'd be willing to bet it wouldn't have been that hard to find out he's at the St. Regis even if we didn't have you, José, am I right?"

José looked at Lawson. "He's not wrong."

"And you said you have a daughter, right?" King took a couple of steps toward Lawson.

"Yes, but I can't let this monster get away with killing Brittany. I can't have my daughter ask me what I did about her babysitter's death and tell her I could have stepped in, but did nothing."

"Better than a couple of police officers showing up at your door to tell your daughter that you're dead."

Lawson put his hands on his hips, but he didn't have anything to say. It was hard to argue with the ugly truth.

"I've been thinking," King said. "Even though I have two more top-notch agents coming to help us, it's not enough. Years ago I would have run headfirst into this thing— endangering everyone with my recklessness. But boys, this is a raid fit for a full-on military team—not for a few people who have never worked together before—no matter how skilled we are individually."

"So what are you saying, X?" José said, putting his hands on his hips. "We just quit?"

"No, I'm saying we use our heads instead of our hearts. Trust me, it's not something I'm used to."

"So, what then?" Lawson said. "If we don't take out Ortega, how do any of us get what we want?"

King looked at José. "What was the name of the guy you said was making the fake videos of me?"

"Manuel. Manuel Cortez."

"Does he have an army protecting him?" King said.

"No," José said.

"Then we start with him."

"You want the tech guy?" José said.

"No," Lawson answered for King. "He wants the tech guy's computer."

King made a gun with his hand and shot a "correct" air bullet at Lawson.

"I get how that helps you, King," Lawson said. "You find evidence of faking the videos of you on the computer of one of Ortega's men, and the CIA backs off of you. But what about Brittany?" Lawson looked at José. "And wouldn't that leave José here in the wind?"

"Getting the computer is just the first step," King said. "How do you eat an elephant?"

"What?" José said.

"Seriously?" Lawson wasn't amused.

"I know, it seems silly," King said. "But it's true here. We can't take Ortega all at once. It has to be—"

"One bite at a time," José said.

"Glad you caught up there," Lawson said as he gave him a pat on the shoulder.

José shrugged. "I don't like it. I say we hit Ortega while he is in a soft zone at the hotel. The rest will be easy."

"I disagree," Lawson said. "King's right."

"Right about what? It being dangerous?" José said. "Well, no shit. You don't think it's dangerous being an undercover agent with these guys? My entire life is danger."

"Who do you think you're talking to?" King said. He didn't like how much pushback he was getting from José. He understood it—the man's life was hanging in the balance—but he didn't like it.

"Look," Lawson said, turning to José, "I don't have the military experience you have, but that doesn't mean I haven't seen my share of tight spots. And from the sounds of it, King here and I have a lot in common. I used to storm the castle too soon too. Almost got myself, my partner, and my daughter killed in the process. I want Ortega for what he did to a sweet girl, but I don't want to leave my daughter without a father."

"Then you shouldn't have come to Mexico," José said.

King watched as the two men puffed their chests. If this is what he'd looked like to Sam all those times he pushed to race into battle over the years, he owed her an apology. "Men, cool off. We're on the same team and we have the same goals."

"Do we?" José stared a hole through King.

King didn't like being challenged, and he let his ego get the best of him.

"You better watch who you're talking to. Not only am I your superior, but I'll whip your ass."

Just as things began to boil over, King's phone started to

ring. He pulled it from his pocket and saw it was the same number Sam had called from. He held up a finger and answered. He heard some rustling on her end, and for a moment King thought maybe Sam had butt-dialed him. Then he heard Sam's voice. It was far away, like she was standing at the other side of the room, but he managed to hear five words that sent a chill down his spine.

"Where are you taking us?"

23

"Where are you taking us?" Sam said to the four men now escorting her and Kyle up the jetway.

At the entrance back into the airport, airport security looked to be in full cooperation. This meant not only that the men's FBI credentials were real but also that there had been some sort of formal phone call made to the head of airport security from someone in the FBI. Otherwise, they wouldn't have been able to enter the airport with guns so quickly. This didn't mean it was actually someone from the FBI, but whoever these men were, their leader knew the rules and was very meticulous in following them. This made Sam nervous.

"In for questioning," the man holding Sam's arm answered. "Where do you think?"

"Questioning for what exactly?"

Sam wanted to keep the men talking while she tried to figure out her and Kyle's next move. She hoped one of them would say too much and at least give her a clue.

"We know you were on your way to help a wanted fugitive. No reason to play games."

"Kyle and I were on our way to Mexico to get married. I have no idea what you're talking about."

"Okay, *Beverly*." The man looked at Sam and smiled in a way that led her to believe he thought he'd won. This was good. Overconfidence leads to mistakes. She just needed to be ready to capitalize.

The men walked them out into the airport terminal. The crowd gave them a wide breadth as they gawked. She'd already figured whoever was framing Xander was an insider of some sort; this all but proved it. Knowing the inner workings of US politics among government agencies wasn't easy for a foreign enemy. Especially not on this level. It takes some serious balls to fake FBI credentials and pull a CIA agent off an airplane. Whoever was pulling the strings was not only fully capable but also, for whatever reason, fully committed to seeing Alexander King publicly burned at the stake.

Kyle glanced back at her. She knew he was thinking the same thing—*Do we fight them now and try to dodge airport security, or do we wait until we reach the parking lot?* Each option had its disadvantages, but whatever happened, Sam didn't want any innocent people at the airport to die for her poor timing. These men didn't know it yet, but it really was bad luck for them that Kyle had been able to make it to the plane. Without him, she wouldn't have had a chance against all four of them.

The four men urged the two of them along. At some points during their walk the men even received some applause from an adoring but clueless crowd. Sam was in the 90 percent range of certainty that these four men were not actually FBI. But before she murdered them in cold blood, she recognized that she needed to be 100 percent. They walked out into the cool night. The arrivals section just outside baggage claim was bustling. These men wouldn't do anything here, but she needed to know if they were who they said they were or not before she initiated anything.

"This a direct order from FBI Director Phillips?" Sam said.

"None of your business really, but Director *Simmons* did order this directly."

Strike one. Either the man had been told the question might come up or he really was FBI. He knew the correct answer. Was she wrong in thinking they weren't really FBI? Sam always relied on her instincts. Her gut was rarely wrong. And though these men hadn't done anything outright to make her think they were imposters, other than the odd ticks and the wrong standard-issue pistol, she just couldn't shake the feeling.

The man who'd been doing all the talking pulled out his phone.

"Director Simmons, we have them in custody."

This was Sam's only chance. The man continued his conversation as they crossed the street toward the entrance to the short-term parking garage. Everything inside her was telling her not to go with them. She glanced over to the man on her right. As she was about to open her mouth, Kyle glanced back over his shoulder at the same man and cleared his throat.

"You look so familiar. Do I know you? I started in the FBI. Didn't we come up together?"

The man didn't speak. Kyle was taking Sam's tactic and trying it on the other escort.

"I know I know you. I'm sure of it." Kyle kept on. "I trained at Quantico. You train there too? Or were you at Camp Peary?"

Camp Peary is where the CIA trains. Sam was praying the man would fall for the bait just to shut Kyle up.

"Hey, stop talking." The man on the phone covered the receiver to scold Kyle. Then he went back to his call. They walked inside the parking garage. They were running out of time.

"Nah, you were at Quantico with me," Kyle stayed with it. "I remember now. You were the one who used to date that sexy blonde. What was her name? Angie? No, was it Brooke? Help me out here, guy—"

"I don't know you. Now shut up." The man pointed forward toward the two black SUVs. It was now or never.

"No, man. It's you, isn't it? Mark? Hell yeah, man. Remember that one night we—"

"I was at Camp Peary," the man finally said, cutting Kyle off. "You couldn't have known me. Now shut the hell up and get in the truck."

Was it absolute proof these men weren't FBI? No. But Sam knew enough about government agency pride that an FBI agent would never say he was trained at Camp Peary. Even if it was just to shut someone up.

"Really?" Kyle said. "My bad. You look just like *my* Mark."

Sam heard the emphasis on the word *my* and understood why Kyle used the name Mark. She was impressed. Kyle had grown a lot since the last time they'd fought side by side.

Kyle's mark would be the man to Sam's right, so Sam's mark would be the man on the phone as well as the man behind her on her left. As soon as she watched Kyle rotate his hips and fire a left hand at the man next to her, Sam whipped her right foot around and kicked the man on the phone in the stomach. He doubled over as Sam let her momentum carry her right hand toward the man's head behind her, but he ducked and hit her hard in the left side of her stomach.

The man with the phone rose, but before he could pull his pistol, Sam managed to push-kick him hard enough on the hip to send him off balance. When the man who'd hit her came rushing toward her, she spun and he ran right by her. She saw Kyle handling the other two men as the leader she'd kicked reached in his sport coat for his gun. Sam dove at the man who'd just ran by her, tackling him to the ground behind the front of the SUV. As they landed, she reached inside his sport coat but found he didn't have a pistol holstered there. She drove the crown of her head to the man's nose and broke it on impact. This gave her a chance to slip her hand down his back, finding his gun resting there.

"Nice try, but both of you stop right there or I will shoot you!"

Sam peeked from the undercarriage of the SUV, and on the other side of the front tire she saw the leg of the man who'd reached for his gun. Two men were writhing on the ground beyond him—Kyle's victims—and beside them she could see Kyle's legs standing still. She knew the man was holding his gun on Kyle. Sam's was held to the chin of the man with the broken nose. Then she moved the gun out in front of her, beneath the SUV, until the gunman's lone visible leg was in her sights. She squeezed the trigger and blood shot out of the man's knee as he screamed. As she moved her gun back to the man's chin lying beside her, she watched Kyle's legs rush forward and take down the man she'd just shot.

Sam jumped to her feet, keeping her gun on the man with the broken nose. He'd made no attempt to fight her. Kyle rose from the other side of the SUV with a gun in his hand, backing away from the other three men on the ground. They'd managed to turn the tables, but she knew more men would be close by to step in.

"Put him in the back and find something to tie him up," Sam said to Kyle as she motioned toward the man with the bloody leg. "The rest of you, I advise you not to move."

As Kyle put the leader of the four men in the back of the SUV, Sam went around collecting weapons. As she did, she heard something—a faint noise coming from somewhere close by. It sounded like someone shouting from the far end of a tunnel.

Her phone. She'd forgotten that she'd dialed King and left it in her pocket for him to hear.

Sam walked over and opened the driver door of the SUV and tossed in all the guns she'd collected except for her own. She turned back toward the three men. "Get together now and don't move."

They all huddled in a line. Sam held her gun on them while she removed her phone from her back pocket.

"Xander? Are you there?"

24

After a frightening few minutes of listening to muffled voices leading up to gunshots, King finally heard Sam's voice on the phone.

"Xander? Are you there?"

"Sam! What the hell is going on?"

"We're not going to make it to Mexico City tonight. Four men posing as FBI just removed us from the plane."

"What? *Posing* as FBI? How is that possible?"

"I don't know yet. Kyle and I have them alive. I'm about to start demanding answers. You're in real trouble here, X. This thing runs deep. Whoever is pulling the strings knows what they're doing, and they know how to bypass government agencies. And they know enough not only to be watching you but to be watching your friends."

That last statement brought King a deep feeling of unrest. It also brought back some horrible memories from the last time his friends were known and in danger. That time resulted in him faking his own death. He wasn't going that route again. He'd die for real before he let that happen.

"Both of you are all right?"

"We're fine. You'd be proud of Kyle. He isn't the horny manslut you left two years ago. He now has a quick wit to go with the combat skills you taught him."

"Well, don't tell him that. His head will still blow up like a balloon," King said. "Listen, Sam, I'm in a real spot here without you. I need to know who is doing this if it isn't Ortega acting alone."

"Well, Ortega might be after you, X, but he's not the one in charge. I'd bet Kyle's life on it that it is someone from our side."

"An American?"

"Yes," Sam said.

"I know I've made a lot of enemies, but an American? Who would want not just to kill me but to ruin all the work I've ever done for my country by making me look like a traitor? I'm at a loss."

"I know. I'll get what I can out of these minions, then report back. And I have to call Director Lucas. If the reality of these men posing as federal agents doesn't prove you're not to blame, I don't know what will. What's your next move there?"

"It was to go after Ortega, but I think I'll go for the computer where these fake videos were made. At least I'll have some proof it wasn't really me."

"I like that. Keep me posted. I'll be in touch."

Sam ended the call. King had walked into José's bedroom to listen to the call from Sam. He hadn't bothered turning on the lights. He took a seat at the foot of the bed and let out a sigh. He couldn't believe the lengths someone was willing to go to make sure he was made out to be a traitor. Before he could take yet another look into the past to try to figure who was after him, Lawson's shadow filled up the doorway.

"Everything all right?"

The big man clicked on the light switch close to the door.

King's phone vibrated in his hand. It was a text from Dbie:

Lawson Raines is former FBI but a PI now in OC like you said. Went to prison for the murder of his wife in Vegas a long time ago. Got pardoned and took down an entire crime ring. That's all I got.

King looked up and answered Lawson. "No. Nothing is all right. My friends got taken off the plane by some fake FBI agents."

Lawson looked confused. "Fake FBI in a federal airport? Good God. Who the hell did you piss off to get into this kind of trouble?"

"I know, right?"

Lawson glanced back out the door, then walked on inside. "Listen, I know a little about you just from being a curious citizen over the years. When you supposedly died a couple of years back, they talked about a lot of the things you did for our country. I didn't want to believe it could have been you who kidnapped Brittany. And I really didn't until I saw her with you driving out of the airport. I'm sure I don't know a hundredth of the shit you've been through, but I just want to say I'm sorry for what happened back in that parking lot. That was a man fueled by past circumstances of my own, and I—"

"You don't need to apologize, Lawson. Just promise me you'll fight like that if we find trouble later. I've fought in a lot of hand-to-hands in my day, and that was the toughest

I've been in. You said you learned in prison. How long were you in?"

"Ten years."

"Jesus," King said, not expecting to hear that.

"Yeah."

"Can I ask what happened?"

"Let's just say I know what it's like to be set up."

King nodded. He didn't need more from Lawson. He knew what happened to his wife. "We all have our stories, I suppose. You'll have to tell me that one sometime when we're not running for our lives."

"It's not a happy tale. Needless to say, it's what ended my FBI career in Vegas."

"You get the chance to make it right?" King said.

"People paid for what they did, but it will never be made right."

"I hear you. Now you're a PI in the OC? California is a long way from Kentucky. And I don't mean distance."

"You're telling me." Lawson leaned back against the wall.

"I used to have a place in San Diego. Back before I 'died.'"

"I didn't have a funeral like you did," Lawson said, "but the old me died in that prison cell. So I can relate."

King was quiet for a moment. Lawson walked back to the door and looked out into the hallway again.

"What is it?" King asked. "You seem paranoid."

Lawson turned back toward King and lowered his voice. "How well do you know José?"

King was genuinely surprised by the question. His answer was knee-jerk. "Well enough to know he's good people. Why?"

Lawson winced a bit. "I don't know. Can't really say. Just enough of a vibe to ask."

"We have a lot of things to worry about, but José isn't one of them."

"Just trying to put our ducks in a row. So what do you want to do now that we're just a three-man operation?"

José came walking in with haste. "You guys holding a private meeting for a reason?"

King stood. "Good God, you guys need to chill. I understand we're in a tough position, but let's take it easy on the paranoia. Both of you."

Lawson and José looked at each other for a long moment.

"Like I was telling Lawson," King said, "my agents have been delayed. It's just the three of us tonight. That is, if you two are still dead set on fighting a fight that isn't yours."

"I just got off the phone with one of my subordinates." José answered King's question by ignoring it. "He told me where Manuel and his computer are tonight. Apparently he's celebrating his video of you making national news at a strip club not too far from here."

"Why does it always have to be a strip club?" Lawson said. "Can't a gangster get a girl naked without paying for it?"

"This good or bad that he's at this club?" King said.

"It's a really seedy place."

"Shocker," Lawson said.

"Yeah," José laughed. "Seedy here isn't like seedy in the US. It'll be packed with itchy trigger fingers with short tempers. And you'll be the only white dudes in there."

King put his hands on his hips. "Okay, that good or bad?"

"Great, if you're looking for a fight."

"Do we even need to go in?" Lawson said.

"What do you mean?" José said.

"Who carries a laptop into a strip club? Don't you know what his car looks like? We can just break in and take it in the parking lot."

"A man who gets paid only to do tech for a crime boss probably carries his laptop into a strip club. And he won't be out in the main area. He'll be in a private room."

"I'm confused," King said. "If what you're saying is true, they'll never even let us white boys in." King motioned between him and Lawson. "Much less let us in his private room. So again, is this good or bad?"

"Good for me," José said. "They'll lead me right to him. You guys can just wait in the car. Then can we go take down Ortega?" José gave Lawson a pat on the shoulder as he walked out the door. "I'm gonna need some more tequila before we go. And while you two were chatting, I took the weapons out to the car. We're good to go."

King smirked at Lawson. "Still think José's not on our team?"

Lawson shrugged, conveying a whatever-you-say attitude. "Got any more bourbon?"

25

Sam had driven about fifteen minutes from the airport before she turned the SUV into a Walmart parking lot. The lot was filled with cars, but she found a few empty spaces at the far end beneath a glowing streetlight. The sky was black beyond the light now. Time was running out for Sam to find out what the hell was going on. She'd just ended an anonymous call to the DC police, informing them that in the short-term parking garage at the airport there were three subdued criminals tied to the running board of a red Ford F-150. It wasn't an easy phone call due to the moans coming from the man with the hole in his leg in the backseat, but she got it done.

Sam parked the car and dialed CIA headquarters. "Robert Lucas, please," she said to the woman who'd answered.

"I'm sorry, he's not taking calls right now. You can try back—"

"Tell him it's Samantha Harrison. Trust me, he'll take the call."

Out of the corner of her eye, she saw Kyle smirk.

"Going by Samantha now, are we?" Kyle said. "What else has changed since the last time I saw you?"

Sam would like to say she hated the way Kyle was always riding her, but honestly she'd missed him and Xander giving her hell all the time. Like two brothers picking on their sister. Sam rolled her eyes and tuned into the elevator hold music playing in her ear. The CIA couldn't be more of a bore.

"Sam, where the hell are you?" Director Lucas interrupted the sleepy music with a growl.

"Thanks to you, I'm not in Mexico City helping our teammate in the fight of his life."

"Don't, Sam. What the hell is going on?"

"Kyle Hamilton and I just got pulled off a plane headed to Mexico—"

"You were fleeing the country?" Lucas interrupted.

Sam didn't waver. "By four men claiming to be FBI."

"FBI? How would they know where you were?"

"Exactly. That's why one of them is in the backseat of my car with a hole in his leg. I am calling to inform you that you need to get on board finally and understand that King is being set up."

"Where are you, Sam? Come in to the office and let's talk."

"Okay. But I need a favor first."

"No favors, Sam. You are the fugitive here, remember?"

"Okay, Robert, if you believe that, then this call is over. I'll find a way to help Xander on my own."

She heard Lucas take a deep breath.

"What do you want, Sam?"

"This will help us both, so untwist your knickers. I took

the FBI credentials from the four men we escaped from. Run them and find out who they are—or at least who they are not—so we can end this nonsense and go help our friend."

"Okay, Sam. But just because men pose as FBI agents and pull you off a plane to keep you from getting to Xander doesn't mean he is innocent."

"No?" Sam said. "Because I think that is precisely what that means. They will be one of the many clues you've had to show you Xander did not do this."

"You mean like video evidence?" Lucas said.

"We still doing this? It's not 1999, Robert. Those videos are easily faked and you know it. Run these credentials and you'll see."

"All right. I'll call FBI Director Simmons directly to run them and see if he gave any such order."

"You know he didn't. This is just a formality."

"Maybe, Sam. But it's an important one. So you'd better hope you're right."

Sam read off the names of the four men from the credentials in her lap and ended the call.

"You think it's enough for the CIA to call off the dogs?" Kyle asked.

"If we're right about these guys, it will be."

"You think they could actually be FBI?"

"No," Sam said with confidence. "But the first rule in espionage is that you are rarely right about someone."

Sam turned toward the backseat. The man, strapped in by the seat belt, was sweating in his suit, his hands tied behind his back. Blood was running onto the tan carpet below his injured right leg. Kyle reached back and undid the tie that kept the sock stuffed in the man's mouth.

"As you heard, I'm in direct communication with the CIA," Sam said. "So we're going to know who you really are in a matter of minutes. It's up to you if you live to hear the director call me back to tell me if you are a liar or not."

The man laughed. "You're not going to be happy with what you find out."

"So you really are FBI?" Kyle said.

"He might be FBI," Sam said. "But he isn't acting on their behalf. Not tonight."

The man shot her a look that was covered with a smile. "You don't know shit."

"No, I don't know that. But I do know that you will be dead if you don't tell me who hired you. You can try to keep playing your game, but it will lead to you lying in this parking lot with your balls in your mouth and your teeth on the blacktop."

Sam felt Kyle look at her in shock. Fortunately, the man in the backseat was staring into her eyes. She knew he could tell she meant it.

"You have no way out of this," Sam told him. "You're either dead here and now because you didn't tell me what I need to know, or the CIA will put you away for treason. So now it's your choice how you want this to go."

"I am FBI Special Agent Steven Richards," the man said with full sincerity. "You kill me, both of you will spend the rest of your lives in jail."

Not the answer Sam wanted. And it was said in a way she really didn't like—with truth.

"Bullshit," Kyle said. But before Steven could say anything in response, Sam reached back and jammed a knife into the top of the man's thigh. The man screeched in pain, but his hands were tied, so the knife stayed standing in his quadricep muscle.

"Sam?" Kyle said. "What the hell are you doing?"

Sam ignored him and spoke directly to Richards. "Right now you aren't in any danger." Sam reached forward and wrapped her hand around the handle of the knife. "But when I pull this blade just a couple of inches to your inner thigh, right through the femoral artery, you'll be dead in a matter of minutes. You sure you want to keep playing games?"

That got the man's attention. He no longer wore a spiteful smile. Suddenly he looked horrified. Kyle was speechless.

"Your move, boss," Sam said as she sliced the blade a little toward the man's inner thigh.

The man screamed in pain.

Sam's phone began to ring. Richards was in too much pain for his face to give anything away about what she was about to hear.

Sam removed her hand from the knife and answered the phone by putting it on speaker. "And?"

"*And,*" Director Lucas said, "Steven Richards is who he says he is."

Kyle whipped his head around in shock. Sam was holding the same expression.

"But . . ." Lucas spoke again. "Director Simmons didn't give any such orders, and the other three men are not FBI."

Just before Steven Richards began to plead his case, Sam ended the call so Director Lucas wouldn't hear what happened next. This man in the backseat had been sent by the person responsible for King being in danger, and Sam wasn't letting him leave until she knew exactly who she was dealing with.

26

José turned into the parking lot of Queen's Mexico. It was actually more understated for a strip club than King had imagined. He was waiting to see the neon naked lady sign out front, but instead, he saw the golden Queen's logo. The parking lot was full, even at that early hour.

"There's Manuel's Impala right there. He's here."

King looked around and noticed a mostly empty parking lot across the street. "Park over there. We can see the entire place from there."

"I don't want to look suspicious," José said.

"More suspicious than two white men sitting in the car of a strip club parking lot in Mexico City?" Lawson said.

"Good point." José pulled across the street and parked facing the club. "I won't be long, but if I come with trouble, you have all the firepower you need next to Lawson."

King looked back. Their small stack of a twelve-gauge shotgun, two suppressed Daniel Defense AR pistols, and an AK-47 were sitting in the seat. "Yeah, I think we're good."

"They are locked and loaded, so just pick 'em up and shoot," José said as he tucked his pistol in the back of his jeans.

"Thought you weren't expecting trouble?" Lawson beat King to the words.

"Plan for the worst, hope for the best." José got out and began walking toward the club.

The two of them watched José enter. King did a perimeter check. There was light traffic in this part of the city. Not a whole lot of other businesses on their particular corner. On his right, across the street were all residential apartments. The weather was decent, so several people were out walking the streets. King thought of Cali. He wondered how her travel was going. Then he wondered if he would ever see her again. He *really* liked her. But that hadn't meant a thing with other women in his past. Product of the job. It was hard to stay with a man who was never around and who was always in danger.

Lawson was in the back, talking on the phone to his partner, checking on his daughter and asking Cassie if she would look into the things Dbie was currently investigating.

Like he did on a regular basis, King thought of Natalie Rockwell. She was the one woman he'd never been able to forget. Usually, thinking about her made him homesick, because his memories with her were at the Kentucky Derby, then at his home that night in celebration. There were a lot of things he loved about her, but five years later, whenever he closed his eyes, he saw her smile. It was a smile everyone in the room noticed wherever she went.

Then his mind would always jump, as it did then, to the memory of her in his hallway, on her knees, sobbing as the man in black held a gun to her head. After that image he would do his best to forget she existed all over again. But it never worked. She always came back to haunt him. Her laugh. Her touch. That's when he wondered if she was the woman in his mind when Lawson was choking the life out of him. Was she the one silhouetted in sunlight holding his baby? King rubbed his hands across his face and scolded himself for thinking of her. Then he did what he always did when thoughts of her came around. He wished her well in his mind, hoping that she found love and that she was happy. It was all a man from the shadows could do for the woman he loved.

"I said, is there any update from your partner?" Lawson said.

King shook the thoughts floating in his mind and turned in his seat to face Lawson. "No. Everything okay back in Orange County?"

"Yeah. All good. My partner said Senator McKinley's been calling. She's taken at least three shouting phone calls from him."

"Well, the man did just lose his daughter. I suppose he's allowed that."

"Yeah," Lawson said as he picked up one of the AR pistols lying in the seat beside him. "I just hate that Cassie has to be the one to hear it, since I'm the one responsible for her not coming home."

"You can't think like that," King said. "You did all you could. We are in the hornets' nest right now, and it was a place Brittany never should have been. Pretty impressive you tracked her down at all."

Lawson was moving the AR pistol around in his hand. "Speaking of impressive, these things are light as hell."

King strained his eyes in the dark to see if the magazine

was inserted. "Yeah, those make great truck guns. Light—only a 7.5-inch barrel, which is good for maneuverability. Depending on the setup and if it's loaded, they're usually only around six pounds."

"Don't think this one weighs six pounds," Lawson said. Then he set it down and picked up the other AR pistol. "This one either."

"Let me see?" King reached out his hand.

Lawson handed the semiautomatic AR to King, and as soon as Lawson let go of the gun, he could tell it was too light. He press-checked and found no round in the chamber. He then ejected the magazine and tilted it into the light.

"It's empty, isn't it?" Lawson said.

King nodded. "Hand me the other AR. Check the shotgun and the AK."

King took the other AR from Lawson and knew before he checked that it, too, was empty. He did his best to keep his mind from jumping to conclusions, but his heart knew of only one. CIA agents don't make mistakes like forgetting the ammo. He knew Lawson's feeling had been right. José had turned on him. The only mistake made here was King's, for trusting someone he barely knew.

"Both empty," Lawson said. "Should we give him the benefit of the doubt? He did say the spare ammo was in the box you carried to the trunk.

"I trusted him. I never even checked it."

"Shit," Lawson said. "Sorry. I know you thought he was your guy."

"No, I'm the one who's sorry. I just got us both killed."

"I still have my Sig and a spare mag," Lawson said.

King stared at Lawson for a moment. Two things ran through his mind. First, Lawson wasn't afraid of dying in the slightest. He could see that right through the man's cold eyes. Two, and much more importantly, he thought about the box in the trunk, followed by José's plan to leave the two of them alone in the car. Then it hit him.

"Get out!" King shouted as he grabbed his go bag and reached for the door handle. "Get out of the car and run!"

King bolted forward as soon as his shoes hit the pavement. Lawson wasn't far behind. There was no reason to explain to the private investigator that the box in the trunk was a bomb. Lawson slid across the trunk of a nearby car at the same time King slid over its hood. As soon as they both hit the ground, a massive explosion boomed into the air. An orange cloud illuminated everything around them. King peeked back over the car they'd taken cover behind and watched as flames from the ruined Impala stretched toward the black sky above.

Lawson had been right.

José was a rat.

King knew without looking that José and a host of other gun-toting thugs were headed his way from the strip club. The only option now was to retreat. When King looked over at Lawson's face with its fiery-orange glow, he could see the big guy had figured the same.

"Let's get the hell out of here," Lawson said.

"I'm right behind you."

27

In the time that Sam and Kyle had been sitting in the parking lot, her phone had been ringing nonstop. Director Lucas was calling to talk her out of doing damage to the rogue FBI agent in the backseat. The same man who was still whimpering from the knife Sam had jammed into his leg.

"What's the plan here, Sam? We really going to torture this guy right here in the truck?"

Sam looked over and held Kyle's glare. "Yes. That's exactly what we are going to do. Whatever it takes."

Kyle shook his head. Sam knew what was coming. It was the speech she would normally give King for going off script.

"At some point we have to act like we work for the government," Kyle said. "We do have rules we swore by. We aren't above the law."

Sam shifted in her seat toward him. "What do you want to do then, Kyle? How would *you* handle this, Mr. Secret Agent?"

"You don't have to be sarcastic. I'm just trying to be the voice of reason."

The usually hotheaded Kyle had changed in many ways. Sam wasn't used to it, and honestly, she wasn't sure she liked it.

"What happened to you, Kyle? Where's that Hamilton spunk?"

"It died the day you told me my best friend died."

Sam could feel the couple of years' worth of pain shine through in that statement. But it didn't soften her. "Yeah? Well, Xander's alive, and you need to snap out of it. He did what he did to keep you safe—"

"Bullshit—"

"He did it to keep you safe!" she matched his rising tone. "Whether it was or was not the right thing to do, that was his intent. And you know it. So stop moping around and help me return the favor!"

Kyle was taken aback by the way she pressed him with such vigor.

Sam's burner phone rang again. "What?" she shouted.

"Sam." It was Director Lucas. "Bring Agent Richards here to headquarters, unharmed, right now."

"Why, so you can drag this out for a few days, hold Kyle and me hostage, and then receive news of how Alexander King was killed in action because you won't let me do what I do?"

"Sam, I am not asking. Bring him here. That is an order."

Sam looked up at Kyle. He was clearly concerned, but what she hoped was really behind those eyes was a willingness to do whatever it took to get Xander. Sam glanced back at Agent Richards. She knew he was the only way she could possibly get some information that could move her at least a little closer to the person responsible for making King the most wanted man alive. And that wasn't going to happen by following orders.

"Robert, you said it yourself, I am the fugitive here. Just let it be known that Kyle had nothing to do with this."

She heard Director Lucas shout her name just as she ended the call. Agent Richards's whimpering heightened.

"Things are different now, Sam," Kyle said. "This isn't like when we went after the man who killed Xander's parents. I was just his buddy then. I am an agent now. I swore an oath to my country."

Sam couldn't believe her ears. This was the last thing she ever expected from Kyle. She knew how much he loved Xander, but she couldn't fathom his current frame of mind. Maybe Xander not confiding in Kyle that he wasn't really dead had actually broken something in Kyle. A trust and bond they'd had. Maybe Kyle felt so betrayed by being kept out of the loop that he couldn't make his way back. Either way, Sam couldn't let that affect what she needed to do. She was not going to be derailed.

Sam made sure Kyle was looking at her when she turned in her seat to face him. "Then get the hell out of the truck, *Agent* Hamilton."

Sam could feel herself go cold. No matter what happened, she would never look at Kyle the same way again. He was dead to her.

"I said, get the hell out of the truck!"

Her shout was so loud that Kyle jerked back.

"Go! Now!"

He jerked again, then slid his hand down to the handle. Sam turned her attention to the man in the backseat as she once again grabbed ahold of the handle of the knife. "Who hired you? Tell me now or I will slowly and methodically drag this blade through your leg until every ounce of blood in your body is in a pool at your feet."

The man began breathing hard, but he did not speak.

Sam pulled the knife to her left. She could feel the blade tearing through muscle and flesh with each millimeter of movement. In her focus she vaguely heard the passenger-side door shut beside her. In her peripheral vision, she could see that the seat next to her was empty. Kyle was gone. But her resolve was not. The man screamed in pain. The blood began to pour freely from the open wound.

She continued to drag the knife as she spoke again. Her voice was cold and calm. "Give me a name, or you die."

She moved the knife a little more.

"I'm running out of real estate."

The man began groaning in pain. He spoke through gritted teeth. "Either way I'm dead, so what's the use?"

Sam remained calm. "You may be right, but if you live now, you at least have a chance to disappear. You tell me who hired you and I promise you won't die here."

"Why should I believe you?" The man was at his wits' end.

"I don't care if you believe me or not. Your only chance at living is to talk."

Along with continuing the steady movement toward the femoral artery, Sam slowly began to give the knife a twist.

"Okay! Stop! I'll tell you everything I know, just stop!"

Sam let go of the knife. The inside of the SUV had become stifling. She flipped on the air conditioning, turned backed to Richards, and folded her arms—ready to listen.

28

The man stared at Sam folding her arms as he took a second to catch his breath. Sam let him. She didn't want to miss a word. The SUV had the metallic smell of blood but had at least cooled a little since she upped the air conditioning.

Agent Richards finally spoke. "Just a couple of hours ago, when I went out to my car, there was an envelope on the console with ten grand and a burner phone in it. I opened it, and there was an unread text message. It was a picture of my daughter at her school. The text with it said I do everything I'm asked or she dies. Reply with yes. When I texted yes back to the number, I got a new text with the post office's address and a PO box number. I wasn't going to respond, but when the next text said that the key to the PO box is in my daughter's dresser drawer in her room, I didn't have a choice. Someone had been in my daughter's room. What was I supposed to do?"

"I don't care what you were supposed to do. I just want

to know what you did and who the person was telling you to do it."

Agent Richards took another deep breath as he looked down at his bloody leg. "There was an envelope in the PO box with three fake FBI credentials and directions on where to meet the three men you saw at the airport and what to do after I had you."

"What were you supposed to do?"

The agent hesitated for a moment. "Full disclosure? I was supposed to kill you. But I swear to God I would never have done it."

Sam laughed. "Yeah, well, I guess we'll never know now, will we?"

The agent didn't speak.

"So the instructions were to find me and kill me? How'd you find me?"

"Whoever was texting knew you'd go to the airport. And they must be well connected because they said they could coordinate with airport security to let us pass."

Richards laid his head back against the headrest and stared at the ceiling. "Please don't kill me. I just wanted to keep my daughter safe." He looked at her. "You understand that, don't you? Aren't you just trying to keep someone safe?"

Sam bypassed the question. "I still haven't heard you say who set all this up."

"I have no idea. I promise you. Like I said, they must be well connected, but the texts were all the communication I had. Please. Check the phone in my pocket. The texts are still there."

Sam reached into his left pocket and pulled out the phone. She opened it and moved to the messaging app.

There was only one contact in the text threads. She clicked on it, and every text he talked about was there, exactly the way he had described them. Then the last text from whoever was in charge was telling Richards to confirm when the job was done.

Sam looked up at Richards. "Something isn't adding up, Agent," she said. "You went through all of this because of a little money and a threat sent by text?"

"And the key in my daughter's room."

"Okay, but you're FBI. You know how to protect your daughter from this sort of threat. Why do all of this blind? There is something you aren't telling me."

Sam closed the messages app and tapped her finger on the green phone icon. There were no phone calls made. She tossed the phone back in the seat beside Richards and retook her grip on the knife in his leg. He screeched in pain.

"Tell me what you're leaving out or you're dead. I don't have time for games."

"Okay! Stop! It was nothing of consequence to you," Richards said, then took in a deep breath. "It was just another picture. It was me with another woman. They sent it to my personal phone. That's it. They were threatening to take my entire life from me. I didn't have a choice!"

"There's always a choice," Sam said.

"Yeah, and I made mine to protect my family. If you can't understand that, then go ahead and do what you're going to do anyway. But I'm not the enemy. Whoever it is that wanted you, they are connected somewhere. FBI, CIA, DOJ, I don't know, but somebody high up has a hard-on for you or whoever you're trying to help. I'm just someone caught in the middle."

Sam knew he was right, and when Richards said the

acronym CIA, the hair on the back of her neck stood on end. At no point had she suspected someone like Director Lucas was involved. But how things were playing out— Lucas detaining her, Richards explaining that this person pulling the strings was clearly connected—she had no choice but at least to take a second look. What didn't make sense about Director Lucas—besides a lack of motive—was why would he go through a second party to stop Sam from getting on the plane? He could have had the real FBI do it.

There were a lot of questions and no clear answers. And that was terrible news seeing as how King was stuck in the thick of it down in Mexico City. She had to get there. She could worry about the rest once King was safe. Meanwhile, she was going to have to shake the fact that Kyle wasn't the man she'd thought he was. She had no idea how she was going to tell Xander that Kyle had abandoned him.

Sam exited the SUV and went around to the agent's door. She opened it and untied the mess of seat belt Kyle had used to subdue him. Richards got out without being told. She shut the door and went back to the driver's side. She took a deep breath and looked up into the darkness beyond the parking lot's light. Of all the things that had happened today, Kyle's betrayal was the hardest to swallow. It affected her to her core.

She heard the burner phone ringing inside the SUV. She grabbed it and saw it was Kyle. She ignored the call and got inside. A text message followed immediately from him. It said, "Just call me, Sam. It's not what you think."

Sam hesitated, then did what he asked.

"Hello," Kyle answered.

"Don't waste my time."

"Meet me at Montgomery County Airpark," Kyle said. "Now."

"I'm not meeting you anywhere."

"Sam! Don't be shortsighted. You know I would never leave X in the wind. Me leaving you in that car hedged our bets when you let Richards go. And you already did, didn't you?"

Sam watched in her rearview mirror as Richards limped off into the dark of the parking lot.

"What are you getting at, Kyle?"

Sam couldn't help but already feel a sense of relief, even though she had no idea what Kyle was going to say.

"I have an old King's Ransom Bourbon corporate credit card that Xander gave me. I just chartered a plane with it under one of the fake passports you always told me to keep handy just in case. This is that 'just in case.' Let's go get our friend out of trouble."

Sam was nearly moved to tears. She hadn't heard sweeter words in quite some time.

"Good to have you back."

"I never left. It was you and X who left me out."

Sam was gutted for doubting him. And for advising Xander years ago not to let Kyle know he was alive. But she didn't show it. "I'm on my way."

29

Alexander King and Lawson Raines had only been running for a couple of blocks when two cars skidded to a halt on the road in front of them, blocking their immediate path of escape. The fire had still been burning from the car explosion behind them, and just beyond that was a gang of Raúl Ortega's men, heavily armed and being led by José Ramirez.

Clearly King had been wrong about him.

When the gunmen popped out of their two cars in front of them, King and Lawson were forced to run left down an alley. What King hadn't expected was for that alley to be a dead end. The two of them took cover behind a large dumpster, then watched as the gang of drug and human traffickers entered the alley, essentially blocking them in.

"Special Ops teach you how to get out of a mess like this?" Lawson asked, his gun pointed around the dumpster at the men filing in.

"Of course," King said.

"And?"

"Easy. Don't get yourself in a situation like this."

"Damn good training," Lawson said. "Yet here we are."

King felt his phone vibrating in his pocket. This was at least the third time it had rung since they'd avoided the bomb in the car. But he couldn't worry about who it was right then. He had to concentrate on staying alive.

The alley was dimly lit by a few scattered lights from the windows of local residents. It was enough to see that there were at least ten or so men now taking root about fifty yards from them.

"I've got thirty rounds," King said. "But I don't think that's going to be enough. We have no angle here."

"I count maybe a dozen of them. They'll drive back here first and use the car for cover. There's a door about fifteen yards up on our left. Two more on our side here about ten and twenty feet. But we have no cover."

"And cover fire will only keep maybe half the alley from shooting."

"It's over, Xander." José's voice echoed down the alley. "We can do this the hard way or the easy way. My boss would prefer to have you alive, but ultimately he'll take what he can get."

King was happy to talk. Maybe it would stall things enough to give him time to come up with an exit strategy.

"That right?" King shouted back. "And just *who* exactly is this *he* you're taking orders from?"

"Raúl Ortega. But you already know that."

"Do I?" King said. Then he whispered to Lawson, "Any ideas?" Then back to José. "What's the motive, José? He doesn't even know me. Why would he care about framing me to look like a traitor?"

"Not my concern, X. Now come on out, or I'm sending my men down."

"Okay, José. You've seen me in combat. Send them down. You know they won't make it back."

Lawson leaned over and whispered, "I think we go for the door." He nodded in the direction of the door fifteen yards to their left.

"Not this time, King," José said. "No way out."

"I bet you thought that about the car bomb, too, right?"

"Maybe, but this is far worse. You're trapped. Let's save some bullets and come on out. I'm not going to ask you again."

King looked at Lawson. "What if the door is locked?"

Lawson glanced down at his shoulder, which was massive even in a button-down shirt. "Let me worry about the door. You give me as much cover as you can."

King believed Lawson that he absolutely could take down that door, even if it was locked. Lawson handed King his Sig Sauer and readied himself for a run.

King readied both guns before talking to José. "All right. I've run all the scenarios, and you're right. There's no way out for us. I am going to ask you one last time not to do this, José. From one frogman to another. No amount of money can change that we're brothers."

"Money changes everything, X. Especially when your own government doesn't take care of you."

King had heard that line a hundred times over the years and even felt it himself sometimes. But as a SEAL you don't sign up to be treated fairly; you sign up to do whatever you're told so you can keep your country safe.

"I hear you," King said. Then he whispered to Lawson,

"I'll shoot when you take off." Back to José, he said, "If it's money you want, you know I can get you plenty."

King's phone continued to vibrate in his pocket.

"Yeah, I know, X. And I'll spend it all from my jail cell, right?"

Lawson shot out from behind the dumpster toward the door. King began running as he fired both pistols, one at the left side of the alley, the other at the right. The men at the far end ducked for cover out of surprise. This gave Lawson enough time to reach the door. He lowered his shoulder like a rhino approaching its prey, and the door exploded inward. Return fire began from the mouth of the alley, and King fired off the last of his rounds as he dove for the open doorway.

As soon as King's stomach hit the ground, he felt a pull at the back of his pants. Lawson had lifted him back up to his feet, and the two of them were running through the hallway of a rental complex. A woman up ahead on the left let out a scream, and Lawson nearly put a man on their right through a wall as he made a hole for King. As if relaying a baton, King handed Lawson his pistol. They both replaced their empty magazines and ran for the other end of the hallway, but King could see up ahead that there was no door.

"Is there a back exit?" King shouted at a man, but the man didn't respond.

"This way!" Lawson shouted as he turned left.

King followed down a short hallway that led to a door. Lawson was a bull in a china shop and continued right through the door and on out into a parking garage. A woman was pulling up in a small red sedan, and for the second time that day King was involved in a carjacking. The woman handed the keys to Lawson without a fight once he held his gun out to his side. King hopped in the passenger seat as Lawson got in and started driving forward. There were groceries in the back. King was leaving quite a wake on his trip to Mexico, something a day ago he never thought would be the case.

The tires spun as Lawson pulled away.

"Go out and make a left in the opposite direction of José and men. Hopefully we can make it out in time."

The exit was just in front of them now. The phone continued to vibrate in King's pocket. He couldn't stand it any longer; he had to find out who it was. Just as he pulled the phone from his pocket, headlights filled the driver-side window as they exited the parking garage. A truck slammed into the side of their car, sending it spinning out into the main road. Glass shattered all around them, and Lawson, wearing no seat belt, was thrown on top of King.

After a couple more spins, the car finally came to a stop. King scanned the surrounding area as he pushed Lawson back over into his seat. There were billboards and lights everywhere above them, so much so it almost seemed to be daylight. A few more vehicles screeched to a stop around them.

"You okay?" King said.

Lawson reached down in the floorboard and picked up his gun as he looked out the front windshield at the two trucks in front of them. "For now."

"José said Ortega preferred me alive."

"You believe that?"

"No. But what choice do we have?" King nodded to his right as two more trucks came to an abrupt stop and José hopped out of one of them.

"No choice, looks like," Lawson agreed. "So we go with them now and look for a better spot to get away?"

"It's the last thing I would ever say we do, but right now it's all we've got. We are wide open here. Hopefully they don't separate us."

They shared a look for a moment that confirmed neither one of them had a better idea.

"Weapons out the window and on the ground," José shouted. There were seven more men around them holding guns. "Get out slow, nothing cute."

King did as asked. He waited for Lawson to push open his indented door; then both of them tossed out their guns and exited slowly.

"Hands up, fellas. Keep them high."

King did as asked. Lawson followed suit. A pit formed in King's stomach as they both reached for the sky. What came next was not going to be fun. He just hoped both he and Lawson could survive.

30

"Both of you to the front of the car," José shouted to King and Lawson.

With their hands still held above their heads, they did as told and walked to the front of the car. King had thrown his Glock forward out the window earlier, so he was only standing a foot or two from it. However, being surrounded by José and his men, it may as well have been a mile.

"You still have time to not be a treasonous prick," King told José. "I won't tell what happened before if you repent now and join the winning team."

"Doesn't look like you're doing a lot of winning right now, King. You should probably just keep your mouth shut."

King looked over at Lawson and found him scanning the area for any possible way out. King had already run all the scenarios. They were trapped. There was no way around it. King's phone continued to vibrate in his pocket. He'd give anything to be able to answer it freely. However, with the way it had been relentlessly ringing, it was bound to be bad news.

"So what now, José? You turn me over to Ortega, and he pays you handsomely? Ups your rank in the gang of degenerates and pedophiles? What's your endgame here, brother?"

The cars coming down both lanes of traffic were making U-turns without protest. It was almost as if running into a gang holding guns was second nature to the citizens of Mexico City. There was one exception. Just a few seconds ago a van pulled to the corner from a side street, and it hadn't moved. Things couldn't get worse for King, so the van wasn't a worry. It was actually more of a hope. Especially when he saw someone get out of the passenger door wearing a cowboy hat.

"My endgame shouldn't be the *end* you're worried about," José said. "Now turn around, both of you, and put your hands on the hood."

King turned and slowly did as asked. He looked back up over José's shoulder, and the cowboy hat was actually walking toward him. King then located his gun on the ground once more—just in case there was a Hail Mary about to be thrown his way.

"No sudden moves, or I will kill both of you," José said. He still had a shotgun trained on King and Lawson, but he had yet to move from the cover of his car. He'd seen what King was capable of before, and he wasn't taking any chances. "Hector, you have the zip ties?"

Hector answered yes.

"You and Juan get out there and tie them up," José ordered.

Two men moved out from behind a different vehicle

toward King and Lawson. King looked back up at José. The cowboy hat was right behind him now. King didn't want to let wishful thinking put him in an even deadlier position, but he couldn't help but think the cowboy was there to help. It was the only thing that made sense.

"Don't let them tie you," King whispered to Lawson.

"Hey!" José shouted. "Shut the hell up! No talking!" José fired a round into the air. The cowboy was at his back. Everyone's attention was drawn to the gunfire. What came next all happened in the blink of an eye.

José's shotgun dropped to the ground as he grunted in pain. King turned just in time to watch Lawson nearly snap the man's arm in half who attempted to tie him up—at almost the same moment when King felt a man's hand around his left wrist. King shot his right hand up for the man's throat and bludgeoned his Adam's apple. Over the man's shoulder, King saw the man in the cowboy hat pick up José's shotgun and blast the man next to José. But suddenly a man raising a gun was behind the cowboy.

King dove across the hood of the car and grabbed his Glock as he landed on the pavement. He twisted over onto his right shoulder and fired three shots at the man raising his gun, dropping him before he could shoot the cowboy. Then King moved his gun to the man he'd just punched and put one in his forehead. Simultaneously, there were gunshots on the other side of the car; Lawson must have pillaged the man with the broken arm for his gun, because he was raising it to fire on the last two men King saw standing.

Just like that, the entire situation had turned. Thanks to the cowboy—and possibly one other helper on the opposite side of the car whom King couldn't see. The last of the gunfire blasted off, and King rose to his feet. Lawson turned to his left and pointed his gun at someone.

"Not another step!" Lawson shouted.

King looked across the car and saw a woman with fiery-red hair walking toward them. He was elated to see Zhanna's familiar face. Then he heard an unmistakable, familiar voice behind him.

"Son, lower that gun," the cowboy said to Lawson. "She just saved your britches."

King looked over and was already smiling when he saw the cowboy's face as he stepped further into the glowing streetlights.

"Jack Bronson," King said. "How the hell did they pull you off the farm to get you down to Mexico City?"

The man tipped his cowboy hat up showing his white-stubbled jaw and sun-aged face. "Well, not for the first time, it was to save your ass."

King walked over and wrapped his arms around Jack. Jack was a former SEAL, then CIA. He was retired the first time King met him when King was hunting his mother's killer. He made a hell of a teammate when King was given his own clandestine group—Team Reign. Jack was one of the best snipers in the navy, and he'd helped King on more than a few hair-raising missions. It had been a couple of years since King had seen him.

King pulled back, took Jack by both shoulders, and gave him a grateful smile. "I must be the redheaded stepchild now if all I get for a savior is you, old man."

"You're alive, ain't ya? And you look pretty good for a dead man," Jack said with a smile. "Speakin' of redheads . . ." He nodded behind King.

King turned and watched as Zhanna walked past Lawson. She was as stunning as ever.

"See," King said to Jack with a wink. "This is more like who should be sent to save me." He turned to Zhanna. "Zhanna, you sure are a sight for sore eyes."

Zhanna skipped the last couple of steps and jumped into King's arms. He couldn't have been happier to see his old Russian friend.

"You as well, my friend," Zhanna said. "Glad we got here in time."

King was about to speak when Lawson interrupted.

"I hate to break up this little reunion, but we're about to have the rest of Ortega's gang on top of us. We need to get the hell out of here."

"Good God, son," Jack said to Lawson. "I don't know where you're from, but I need to know what the hell they're feedin' ya." He turned to King. "Where'd you find this one? Working as The Rock's stunt double?"

King shrugged.

"Get to our van and let's get out of here," Zhanna said. "But grab some of these weapons along the way. They won't be needing them."

So before any more trouble could make it to them on that street, they threw the several guns they could find in the back of the van. Jack jumped in behind the steering wheel, and King took the front passenger seat beside him.

"Where to now, ghosts of missions past?" Jack said as he tipped his cowboy hat.

King didn't answer the question. "How the hell did you two find us?"

"You haven't spoken with Dbie?" Zhanna said.

That's when it hit King. He pulled the phone from his

pocket. It must have been Dbie. There were twenty or so missed calls from her.

"Dbie tracked this phone, didn't she?"

"We called her when I met up with Zhanna at the airport about a half hour ago," Jack said. "She led us right to ya. I gotta say, it was a little nerve-rackin' rolling up here without any guns. Can you believe they just don't let you bring your own into the country?" Jack laughed.

"Well, I appreciate the stupid but brave rescue," King said. "Where'd you get the knife you used on José?"

"They'll let ya buy those at the pawn shop. One back right around the corner. But enough about all that. I'm just happy we could help. Question is, where to now?"

"The strip club around the corner. Something I need back there," King said.

"What, your dignity?" Jack smiled.

"We can't go back there, King," Lawson said. "It's too risky."

King turned in his seat to face Lawson. "Everything from here on in is risky. We're at war. And the only way out of this city is to stay on offense and take the fight to Ortega."

Jack turned to face Lawson as well. "Man of your size ain't afraid of a fight now, are ya?"

Lawson returned Jack's smile with one of his own that said to King, "If they only knew." Then Lawson leaned forward and nodded to King. "Ask him if I'm afraid of a fight?"

Jack and Zhanna both examined King's semibattered face. King shrugged.

Jack grinned from ear to ear. Then he turned back around and started the van. "Well, all right then. Strip club it is."

31

By the time Sam ditched Agent Richards's SUV, hot-wired an adjacent car, and made her way to Montgomery County Airpark, Kyle and the plane he'd chartered were ready to go. It was a Citation I aircraft. Not a large plane, and they would have to stop once for fuel on the way to Mexico City.

Sam broke the silence in the cabin. "You couldn't get a plane that could fly nonstop to Mexico City?"

"Typical," Kyle said. "I bail you out, and instead of saying thanks, you go with giving me shit."

"I'm nothing if not consistent."

Kyle gave a grin. "I was pissed we'd have to stop too. But it was the best I could do for two fugitives on an hour's notice."

The plane was taxiing to the ready position on the runway. They were next in line to take off. They were actually the only ones in line to take off. One of the many perks of a regional private airport.

"We need to talk to X before we take off," Sam said. "You

want to do the honors?"

"No, I don't want our first conversation in two years, after he lied to me, to feel forced."

Sam understood. Just before she dialed King, Director Lucas was calling again. Kyle noticed and snatched the phone from her hand.

"Let me buy us a little time."

"Knock yourself out," Sam said.

"Hello! Who is this?" Kyle said frantically. Sam watched as he fell into character, perfect facial expressions and all. "Director Lucas? Oh, thank God! It's Sam! Please hurry. She's hurt and was taken by Agent Richards! I managed to get away, but I don't know where I am!"

Kyle waited for Director Lucas to say what he had to say.

"Yes, she was bleeding bad in the backseat of his car. He turned the tables on us." He waited a beat. "I don't know where she is. Last I saw her was in a Walmart parking lot. Please find her. He's going to kill her!"

Kyle ended the call and went back to normal as if it were nothing.

"It wasn't Oscar worthy," Sam said. "But it was passable."

Kyle rolled his hand forward and bowed for his less-than-adoring fan. Sam dialed King's burner phone. He answered on the first ring.

"Sam. Everything okay?"

"We're fine. Kyle and I have found a way to get to you. We should be there by midnight to give you some help."

"You're not going to believe this, but I already have help," King said.

"Yes, but the private investigator and José aren't enough. You'll need—"

"José is dead."

"What?" Sam took in a breath. "What happened? Did Ortega's men find you?"

"Well, yeah. Sort of. José was Ortega's man. He turned on me and Lawson. Left us in a car with a bomb. Then he trapped us at gunpoint after we survived that."

"I don't understand," she said. "How is he dead and you are free to talk to me?"

"A cowboy and a Russian walked into a bar—or a gang fight, as the case is here."

"Zhanna?"

"Yeah." Sam could sense King smiling. "And Jack Bronson. He's as charming as ever, by the way."

Sam heard Jack mutter in the background, "Kiss my wrinkled ass."

"But I thought Dbie said he refused to help?"

"Guess he had a change of heart," King said. "I've been told I'm irresistible."

Sam scoffed.

"You just rolled your eyes, didn't you?" King said.

"Bugger off. And you're more irresponsible than irresistible these days. You're not in your prime anymore, Xander."

"The hell you say."

"Anyway. That's great news they have arrived. Lay low. I'll see if I can coordinate to get us some weapons."

"Don't bother. We took plenty off José and crew."

"Where are you now?" Sam asked.

"We were going to try to raid a strip club for the laptop that made the fake videos, but thanks to José's big mouth—pointing out the tech guy's car in the parking lot before he tried to kill us—we checked there first. The moron left the laptop in the car. Zhanna already found the software he used to manipulate the video. I'm in the clear if I can get it back to the States."

The jet's engines began to whirl to life.

"Find somewhere to go for the night," Sam said. "Start formulating a plan. Just because you can get yourself clear of taking the girl doesn't mean you're clear. You had enough drugs at your house in Lexington to start your own distribution center. And there's the matter of finding who is behind all of this. For your sake and for sake of the girl's family. Last time I saw the senator as I was leaving Langley, he had just watched his daughter get murdered on television. Taking down Ortega isn't just to rid the world of another scumbag, it's for answers."

"I'm with you, old girl. Just get down here and let's get Team Reign back together officially. Being a spy and staring death in the face isn't near as much fun on your own. Speaking of, how's Kyle doing?"

"Sore. Can you blame him?"

"No. Maybe you can work on him on the way down?"

"I'll do my best."

"Be safe."

Sam ended the call.

"Sounds like a party," Kyle said, void of exuberance.

"Right up your alley," Sam said.

"Not this kind of party."

"You don't miss him at all?"

Kyle's brow furrowed. Sam knew she had hit a nerve.

"Miss him? That's all I've done is miss him, Sam!"

"I know, I'm sorry."

"For two years! He was closer than my brother. I sat with his sister and his niece and cried for hours after we buried him. It's been hell. Every time something good happened to me, the first person I thought to call was X so I could share it with him. And when I was struggling, all I wanted to do was get a kick in the ass from him to stop me from moping around. But he took that from me. *You* took that from me!"

"He did it to save your life!" Sam had had enough. "You should be showing gratitude! Not sitting here sobbing away to me. Your best friend is alive! Live in that moment. Not how butt-hurt you are by what he had to do to protect you!"

They were both seething. They sat quietly as the jet cruised down the runway, then lifted into the air. The cabin lights dimmed, and Sam's phone began to ring. It was Dbie. Sam answered.

"I can't get ahold of Xander! Have you heard from him? Is he all right?" Dbie was frantic.

"I just spoke with him. He's fine. Zhanna and Jack made it to him."

"Jack? I thought he—"

"He had a change of heart, I suppose," Sam interrupted.

"Is that a plane engine I hear?"

"It is. Kyle and I are on our way to Mexico City."

"Kyle? How'd that happen?"

"Long story, Dbie. Can you do me a favor while I'm traveling?"

"Of course."

"I need to know who might have the ability to reach out on behalf of the FBI. Someone who knows the inner workings enough not only to be able to contact agents but to know the strings to pull to get clearance for a team at the airport."

"Sure. That should be a short list. Do you want to include FBI Director Simmons?"

"Include everyone. An insider is working to trap Xander, and we need to find out who. Sooner rather than later."

"On it. Call me when you land, and I'll let you know what I have."

Sam ended the call. She could tell by Kyle's body language—completely turned away from her toward the window—that he was finished talking. So she closed her eyes and drifted off to sleep. Visions of traitors dancing in her head.

32

"I thought I heard Sam tell you to go somewhere and lay low," Jack said.

"Sam says a lot of things," King said. Then he looked back over his shoulder at Zhanna. "Anything?"

The four of them had driven down to the St. Regis in the middle of downtown. It was a beautiful cylindrical building at the edge of a large roundabout. King could see the fountain in the middle; the water spouting up was lit by a myriad of colored lights. When they were making their way to the hotel, Zhanna had been attempting to bypass the security on the laptop, but as Lawson pointed out, a tech guy wasn't going to make it easy to crack his hardware.

"I can't get in," Zhanna said. "Password probably in Spanish. Not really my strong suit."

King looked over at Lawson. He watched as the big man never stopped studying the entrance to the hotel. It was like he was trying to see right through the walls.

"What in particular are you looking for?" King asked him.

"Nothing in particular. I'm looking in general. At everything. Unless you know what we are looking for, I'll look at all of it."

"Thought we was looking for Mexicans," Jack said.

"We're in Mexico, cowboy," King laughed. "Everyone is Mexican."

"Don't be a smart-ass, son. You know what I mean."

"But do I?"

Zhanna chimed in. "You telling X not to be smart-ass, Jack, is like telling you not to be a redneck."

They all laughed.

"She's got a point," King said.

"Anyone have a camera?" Lawson said from the backseat. Apparently he was the only one working.

Zhanna handed over her phone. "You can zoom by pinching with your fing—"

"I know how it works," Lawson interrupted as he raised the phone to snap pictures. "I have a teenage daughter."

"What do you see?" King said.

"Probably nothing, but this guy just went inside a few minutes ago. Already back out."

King heard Lawson taking several shots. He could tell by the lights under the valet area that the man was Caucasian. That was about it. "How good is the zoom on the camera?"

"It is new phone," Zhanna said. "So pretty good really."

"Yeah, I'm getting close," Lawson said. "But his back is turned, so I can't get his face. Probably nobody anyway."

King watched as the Caucasian man froze when he looked in the direction of their van. The man spun quickly and jumped on a motorcycle.

"That didn't look like nothing," King said. "You ready for a car chase, old man?"

Jack started the van. "I am, but I'm not sure this van is."

The motorcycle zoomed forward, and Jack squealed out of their parking spot, making a right onto the turnabout. He took the first exit to make it onto the same road as the motorcycle that was speeding away.

"Step on it!" King shouted. "This might be our only lead!"

Jack did just that, but the torque on the rented van was being left in the dust by the crotch rocket. King scoured the immediate area for something faster, but he knew by the time he took possession, the motorcycle would be long gone. The van was their only chance.

Jack turned left to follow the bike. He cut it early into oncoming traffic to try to make up some ground. It worked. The motorcycle got wedged in by a few cars trying to turn, and Jack cut back across two lanes, landing right behind the bike. The man found a small gap between cars and steered between them. Then the whine of his engine screamed as he took off. There was no way for Jack to make it clean through that same gap, so he decided to make a new one.

"Hold on!" Jack shouted.

He rammed the van into both cars, splitting them apart, then pushed through. He floored it, and when King looked up, he saw a red light. The motorcycle was looking for a clean way through. One more chance for them to catch up before the man got away for good.

"He's going to fit through that next gap, but we'll never make it," King said.

Jack saw the same thing and once again swung wide out into the oncoming lanes. King grabbed the "Oh shit!" handle above his window and hung on for dear life. Jack swerved left to avoid a truck, then right to avoid an SUV, and he had to slam on the brakes, turn right, then back left to avoid the cross traffic headed through the intersection. He managed to do so without getting them killed, and they found themselves right beside the man on the motorcycle.

King looked down at him, but the man's hat was pulled so low he couldn't get a view of his face. King heard Lawson once again snapping pictures, but Lawson quit when he yelled out to warn everyone.

"He's got a gun!"

King looked again and saw a pistol being brought up in his direction.

"Brakes!" King shouted.

Jack responded quickly, and as King was jerked forward then back by his seat belt, the sound of bullets firing lit up the night. King looked up and watched the man try to reach back and fire again, but he had to swerve to avoid another vehicle. Then the man on the motorcycle jumped forward and sped off into the darkness.

King slammed his fist on the dash.

"Shit, I had to brake. Nothing I could do," Jack said.

King slammed his fist again, then let out a sigh. "Not your fault, Jack. I'd be dead if you hadn't. Everyone okay?"

They all gave a yes.

"Lawson," King said, "not that it matters, but did you get the license plate?"

"Yes. But like you said, it won't matter. That plate won't lead back to whoever the hell that was."

Zhanna undid her seat belt as Jack pulled away from the traffic. "You think that man could be involved with dead girl? Or with setting you up?"

"He's involved in something," King said. "Finding out what will be the impossible part."

King adjusted his seat belt and sat back. "Find us some place to lay low. And don't tell Sam I said to. I don't need another 'I told you so'."

Jack pulled away as Zhanna borrowed King's phone to search for a place to stay. Lawson combed the pictures for anything that might be useful, and King just sat and stewed on the fact that a night was going to go by where the entire world thought he was a human trafficker, a drug dealer, and maybe even a murderer. Though he had never cared what people thought of him, this lie that was so widespread and so much the opposite of his true character, he couldn't escape the fact that it hurt. For the first time since faking his own death, he was beginning to long for the days when he was a ghost to the rest of the world.

33

"Well, son, this ain't the St. Regis, that's for sure," Jack said as he set his carry-on suitcase on the second of the two queen beds in the small hotel room.

Since none of them could use credit cards, all they had to book a room was the cash Sam always left King in his go bag. It was enough for everything they needed—food, water, adjoining rooms. They had a place to regroup off the radar, and that was all King really cared about.

Lawson walked in from the adjoining room. "You couldn't pick a place with minibars?"

King turned to find Lawson in his pants and a white tank undershirt, his arm and chest muscles bulging. "Oh, so you do have a sense of humor?"

"Not really," Lawson said.

Jack walked over and looked Lawson up and down. "You'd better room in here with Xander. Man like you could get Zhanna pregnant from one bed over."

King laughed. "Not you, though, old man?"

Jack took off his cowboy hat and ran his finger through his thinning white hair. "Nah. I've been shootin' blanks for longer than you've been alive."

Zhanna walked in. "Should I get my own room? You three are making me nervous." Then she let a wry smile grow across her face.

"Go ahead and freshen up," King said to the three of them. "If you don't mind, I want to hurry and put our heads together on this. See where we land before Sam and Kyle get here."

Jack grabbed his bag and began moving toward Zhanna's room. "I'll jump in the shower, then run out and get us some food."

"Sounds good, Jack. I'm starving. Thank you," King said. Jack nodded and walked forward. "And Jack?"

Jack turned to face King.

"I know we give each other a lot of shit," King said. "But it's damn good to see you and Zhanna, my friend. Thank you for dropping everything to come here and help me out."

"You'd do the same for me. Besides, I wasn't doin' nothin' but breakin' horses and catchin' up on *Sons of Anarchy*."

"Sounds pretty damn good to me."

"Could be worse. *Sons* is a great show, but the adrenaline I got puttin' that knife in the back of that traitor earlier was just a bit more exciting."

"A bit?"

"Yeah." Jack's smile was wide. "A bit." Jack walked into the other room without another word.

Lawson took a seat at the foot of one of the beds in King's room. He was holding Zhanna's phone in his hand.

"You find anything noteworthy in the pictures you took?" King said.

"I had my partner, Cassie, look into the plates on the motorcycle, but she couldn't get through the Mexican government to run it through the database. It would come up stolen anyway, I'd bet my lack of fortune on it."

"Me too," King said. "Anything else?"

"No shots of his face, couldn't even see the color of his hair," Lawson said as he stood. He walked over to King as he scrolled through pictures. "This probably won't help, but there was this one. At least it was some sort of differentiator."

King took the phone and looked over the picture. It was a shot of the man on the motorcycle as he was aiming his gun at King in the front seat of the van. His arm was stretched out, ready to fire.

"You must have taken this right before Jack hit the brakes. I must be missing what you're seeing. Help me out."

Lawson reached over, placed two fingers on the screen, the spread them apart to zoom in. "I almost missed it myself."

King squinted, and then he noticed it. He absolutely couldn't believe what he saw. He let out a small gasp.

"What?" Lawson said.

The part of the picture Lawson had zoomed in on spot-lighted the man's left hand as he held the gun. The reason he'd zoomed in was because the man had his middle finger on the trigger instead of his index finger. And the reason he was using his middle finger to pull the trigger was because this man didn't have an index finger at all.

"Scott Smith," King said.

"Wait, you know this guy? From a missing finger?"

"I don't know him, but he was with Brittany McKinley and her friend at the club the night she was taken."

Lawson looked off as if searching his mind. "The white guy who was talking to them before the fight started? Cassie sent me the footage, but I don't remember seeing a missing finger."

"I never even saw the video," King said. "But when I asked Brittany to tell me everything about that night, it came up in conversation."

"We know anything about who he is?"

"Dbie found a little bit. He's ex–Navy SEAL. Why he's 'ex' and not 'former' has been redacted in his paperwork. He's been a ghost ever since. No paperwork, no driver's license, nothing."

"Unreal," Lawson said, shaking his head. "Then he's the one who took her. So we at least know that much. But doesn't that mean he's also the one who set you up. You were a SEAL, right? You sure he doesn't have a vendetta against you from back in the day?"

"Clearly he has something out for me, but it isn't from something in my SEAL past. He and I never crossed paths, as far as I know, so I certainly never did him wrong."

"You sleep with his girl without knowing?"

King looked over at Lawson. He was serious. "Well, possibly, back then. But that wouldn't be enough to want to out me and make me look like a traitor."

"You'd hope not, but I'm just dotting *I*s and crossing *T*s looking for answers."

"It's not that. But there has to be something."

"I'll get Cassie on it right away," Lawson said. "Maybe she should coordinate with Dbie. Two minds working together are better than one."

"Agreed. I'll call Dbie."

They both were quiet for a moment. Zhanna walked past the doorway and out of sight. She had only a towel wrapped around her and she was drying her wet hair. King looked over at Lawson and noticed him noticing her.

"Good thing the old man swapped rooms," King smiled. "I don't need you complicating things."

Lawson grinned but with the shake of his head. "Nah. I'm already spoken for."

"Yeah, you might be spoken for, but you're not dead. I could see that by the way you looked at her. She's a beautiful woman, inside and out. That can get even the best of men in trouble."

Lawson nodded. "Let's make our calls and get some rest. I don't have the energy to worry about anything else. I'm not nineteen anymore."

"I hear that."

King handed back the phone after studying the picture one last time. It was nice to have some brotherly conversation. It had been a while. It made him all the more happy that Kyle was on his way to Mexico. But it also made him anxious about how his closest friend was going to act when they finally spoke for the first time. King knew Kyle felt betrayed; he just hoped their long history together would trump all of that in the end.

King pulled out his phone and dialed Dbie. He'd learned long ago not to waste time worrying about things he couldn't control. It's what made him good at continuing forward, even when forward wasn't really an option.

34

King woke from sleep when he heard Lawson on the phone. In the haze of a wonderful dream, he checked the clock; he'd been out for a couple of hours. Before he checked his phone to see if Sam and Kyle were close, he closed his eyes and lingered in the trails of the images he'd just watched behind closed eyes.

He didn't understand why he kept thinking of Natalie. Maybe it was seeing old familiar faces that brought her to his subconscious mind. Maybe it was that since Cali had left, it was easier for his heart to find pictures of what it truly desired. On the other hand, maybe it was the fact that Natalie would know he was actually alive soon because of all the media coverage. The thought of being free to see her again could be opening his mind to the possibility of making the impossible a reality. Either way, the feel of her skin, the smell of her hair, and the taste of her lips were as fresh to him as the day he'd met her. And that was why he knew there was something special about her. At least to him.

King heard Lawson end his call with his partner. He rolled over and checked his phone. He'd missed a couple of calls from Sam and from Dbie. Both followed with texts. Sam was relaying that they'd landed, that Dbie had given her the address to the hotel, and that they would be there shortly. That was twenty minutes ago, so they'd be there in just a few minutes. King was both excited and anxious to see Kyle. He moved through his phone and dialed Dbie.

"There you are," Dbie answered. "Everything okay?"

"Just getting some rest. Anything new on Scott Smith?"

King saw Lawson turn his attention to his conversation with Dbie.

"I was just about to call you again. And yes. I found a back channel into his redacted file."

"What?" King sat up in his bed. Lawson moved over and sat on the edge of the bed across from him. "How? Redacted files are impossible."

"Not when you helped drive the President of the United States and his wife to safety a couple of years ago."

"You called President Gibbons?"

"Well, I called the First Lady. Beth and I talk a few times a week, so it wasn't a big deal."

"You do? How did I not know—okay, so what happened?"

"The first thing she said when I called was how awful it was someone would try to frame you like this. I knew right then she had discussed it with the President and he shared her thoughts. So I knew he would help. You should have called him first, X."

"Maybe, but I used that card in Alaska. Didn't think it would work again."

"You saved his life. It's a forever kind of card."

"Okay, so I'm assuming he quietly got the redacted file to you without it being censored?"

"Yes. X, Scott Smith was a sniper for the SEALs. He's the one who shot Brittany in that video. You know he is."

King's mouth must have dropped open because Lawson sat forward with wide eyes. "What? What did she find out?"

King let it process for a moment. He understood that it made sense Smith was the one who shot Brittany because he was a sniper, but why would the man who kidnapped her go through all the trouble of setting King up just to shoot her in the end?

"What I can't figure out," Dbie continued, "is how this has anything to do with you."

Dbie was on the same page as King.

"Dbie, you're the best. See if you can find a connection between this Scott Smith and Raúl Ortega. And more importantly, see if you can find a connection between Scott Smith and Senator McKinley. The two have got to intersect somewhere. Otherwise, why choose Brittany to kidnap? Why would Smith want to hurt me *and* Senator McKinley? There has to be something there."

"I'm on it. That it?"

"I think that's enough, don't you?"

"Well, that depends," Dbie said.

"On?"

"On whether or not you want to know where Scott Smith is right now?"

King stood on reflex. "You know where he is?"

"I found him on the St. Regis security cameras. Then I followed him with traffic cams throughout the city. Even saw where he took shots at a white van. Know anything about that?"

"Dbie, you just got a raise."

"Good, I need a new car."

"And I just bought you a new car."

"You need to get into trouble more often then," Dbie laughed. "I'll text you the address. And I'll tell you if he leaves."

"You're watching him right now?"

"No, but I'm watching a partial view of his driveway."

"I love you," King said.

"I know."

King ended the call. Lawson stood.

"Dbie found out who killed Brittany. It had to be Smith," King said.

Lawson began pacing the room like a lion in a cage. "Let's go get him. Right now. We can't let him leave."

King recognized himself in Lawson. He, too, was ready to go.

"Sam and Kyle are almost here. Let's just—"

"Have them meet us there," Lawson said when he stopped pacing. "We can't let him get away."

Lawson was right. When you have an enemy's location, you never hesitate. Especially when you don't have to wait for orders.

"Mount up," King said.

"That's what I like to hear!"

35

After King called Sam telling her about the situation with Scott Smith, then texting her the address, he, Lawson, Zhanna, and Jack jumped back in the van and took off. It turned out Sam and Kyle were closer to where Scott Smith was staying, so they rerouted and were about to arrive. King and crew had another six minutes to go because they'd made a pit stop at José's "secret" apartment. They were able to procure two more AR pistols with three extra mags. King also found two extra mags for his Glock, one of which he emptied the bullets from so Lawson could have a full mag for his Sig.

Lawson was driving, and Jack was in the back making sure all the guns were locked and loaded. Zhanna was helping Lawson navigate, and King was on the phone with Dbie.

"No, X, nothing has changed at all. The bike is still sitting out front."

"Anything more on Smith?"

"No. Hey, X?" Dbie said.

"I don't like the sound of that."

"Don't you think you should call Director Lucas? Now that you have the laptop clearing you of the videos and we have what we do on Scott Smith?"

"What do we have on Scott Smith, Dbie?"

She was quiet for a moment. "Nothing concrete, I suppose, but an awful lot of coincidences, don't you think?"

"I don't think they are coincidences, but because nothing is proven, there's nothing I can say to Lucas."

"Then call President Gibbons, X. This is your life on the line here. More than that, this is your legacy. If something happens to you in Mexico City, this may all be pinned on you. It's hard to sit back and watch that be a possibility when there is something you can do."

"I'm not calling the President."

Dbie didn't let up. "You saved his life in Kentucky, X. Then you saved his presidency when you didn't let the virus make it to the lower forty-eight from Alaska. You might think you're square because he helped you obtain some information on your mission, but I assure you he doesn't think you're even. According to Beth, he will never think he's done enough for you. He's probably already been up Director Lucas's ass for hesitating to believe you didn't do this. JUST CALL HIM!"

"ALL RIGHT!" King matched Dbie's intensity. "Jesus. You are a pest."

"Squeaky wheel gets the oil, my dad always said. Now call him."

"Keep an eye on Smith." King ended the call.

"That got animated," Lawson said. "What now?"

King shook his head and opened the phone. Dbie had

already texted him the number he needed to get the President on the phone. "I guess I'm calling the President."

"Oh, you roll like that?" Lawson said.

"Guess so. I'm going to put it on speaker. If there's anything I forget that he may need to know, help me out."

Lawson nodded. "You got it."

King dialed the number. He had no idea what President Gibbons knew about the situation, but he didn't have time to get into specifics. As he had learned over the last year, he and Gibbons spoke the same language, so Gibbons would understand the need for brevity.

"Candace Mitchell," a woman answered.

King recognized the name. She was the President's chief of staff.

"Hi Candace. It's Alexander King. Can I speak to the President, please?"

"Alexander King? As in the traitor on the news?"

Lawson made an "oof" face, as if that one hurt. King rolled his eyes.

"Yeah. That's the one."

"I can get you to the CIA Director or the head of the DOJ, but the President isn't going to take your call. He can't be associated with you right now. No matter your history with him."

"That your executive decision you're making for him?"

"It is. So don't call back."

The call ended.

"That went well," Lawson said.

King dialed Dbie.

"That was quick," she answered.

"You gave me the chief of staff's number."

"Yeah, Beth said it would be the only way to reach the President. He's in foreign policy meetings until late tonight."

"Yeah? Well, she denied my call. Hung up on me."

"Shit. Okay. I heard she's tough. I'll have Beth call her. Stay by your phone."

King ended the call.

"Who is this Beth?" Zhanna said from the backseat."

"The First Lady. We should be getting a call back real soon."

King's phone rang, but it wasn't the President. It was Sam.

"Hey, Sam, you guys there?"

"When was the last time Dbie looked at the traffic camera pointing in Scott Smith's direction?"

King didn't like that question. "Just a minute ago, why?"

"Either a lot has changed in the last minute, or she is watching taped footage, because there are three vehicles parked outside along with a motorcycle where Smith is staying. We just now drove by."

"Damn it, okay. Give me a minute. The President is calling me. I'll explain later."

King ended the call by answering the incoming one. "Hello?"

"Mr. King? It's Candace Mitchell. I have the President for you."

King didn't speak. Candace didn't sound too happy.

"X? That really you?"

"It is, Mr. President. Good to hear your voice."

"Don't do that. It's Bobby to you. And I bet it's good to hear any ally's voice at this point. Look, I know you're in a tight spot. I don't need to know what happened, I just need to know how I can help."

"In short, I need you to talk Director Lucas down. I need him and his people helping me find who's behind this, not wasting time hunting me and my friends down."

"Okay. Anything I can give him to help that along?"

"I know who killed the senator's daughter."

"He the man in the redacted files?" President Gibbons said.

"Yes. We know where he is and we are about to ruin his night."

"Sounds like you're doing okay to me. Won't that solve all your problems?"

"It would if I thought Scott Smith was the one who was trying to frame me. Or should I say the *only* one. But he's not. He doesn't have the FBI connections to be able to pull off something that happened to Sam at the airport."

"Okay, then what can I give Lucas to help you?"

"I need to know why Scott Smith would want Senator McKinley to suffer the loss of a daughter. And I need him to try to find out what someone with FBI connections and Scott Smith have to do with each other. If the two are even connected."

"Well, I don't know if it has anything to do with this Scott Smith, but Senator McKinley himself has FBI connections. He's the chairman of the FBI Oversight Committee."

King's head was starting to ache. "Okay. Well, since it was his daughter who was killed, I doubt that has anything to do with me or Sam's incident at the airport, but I also know from experience never to rule anything out. All right. If you can, just get Lucas to hone in on why Scott Smith could hate Senator McKinley, who could have pulled the FBI stunt at Dulles airport, and if any of those things have any connections down the line to Raúl Ortega."

"I can do that," the President said. "But don't you want me to see who, if any of them, has ties to you? You did have a truckload of dope at your horse farm in Kentucky."

"I think finding that out will have to be on me while I'm down here with Ortega. But it never hurts to ask."

"Speaking of asking, next time, X, call me first. I know you have the country's best interests at heart. Your call is never a bother. I wouldn't be here without you."

"I'd say the same about you," King said. "But I'm pretty resilient."

They two of them had a short laugh. Then Dbie's number came up on his phone as an incoming call.

"I have to go, Bobby. Thanks for the help."

"Give 'em hell."

King switched over to Dbie's call.

"Xander! Something's happened to Sam! I think they're —I don't know—you have to get to them!"

King's stomach dropped.

"Dbie, calm and tell me what happened."

"I don't know what happened! I was telling her that I didn't see the cars in the driveway on my end, just the motorcycle, and then I heard this loud noise. Then —nothing!"

"We're right around the corner!"

King ended the call. "Toss me one of the ARs," he told Jack. "Everyone grab a gun and a backup. Smith tapped the traffic camera with the view of where he's staying. He put a video on loop. Sam said there were a couple of cars there. They were just in an accident or something."

Lawson turned right in the direction of their destination. They were coming from the back side, and it didn't take long to see what Dbie had heard. About a block away, there was an overturned car just off the left side of the road.

"There!" King pointed.

Lawson floored it, and the van wobbled as it turned out on the main road. As they moved closer, King could see tiny sparks in between some headlights about a hundred feet from the car that was turned on its side. Sam and Kyle were taking fire.

"Slam them, Lawson! Zhanna, you and Jack cover me while I get Sam and Kyle!"

Lawson pressed the pedal down as they approached two cars in the middle of the road. The glass splintered in the middle of the van's windshield as the bullets were turned on them. King ducked and moved to the driver-side backseat. Zhanna was in the seat across from him, her window already rolled down with her gun out the window.

Then the van made impact. The crash threw King into the floor, but his hand was on the handle by the time Zhanna began shooting beside him, and he was out the door. Gunfire echoed through the air. King didn't look back; he knew the three of them in the van were capable. Only a few steps toward the overturned car and King could see Sam holding her gun on him as she took cover.

"It's me!" King shouted. "We gotta go!"

As the words left his mouth, he noticed two sets of headlights coming toward him on the road. And they were coming fast. Scott Smith or Raúl Ortega—whoever was in charge—had already called for reinforcements.

The mission had just turned from assassination to all-out war.

36

The two vehicles speeding King's way came to a screeching stop about twenty-five yards in front of him. That was when Kyle popped up, and for the first time in over two years, King locked eyes with his best friend. The circumstances for a reunion could not have been worse, so King had to focus on keeping Kyle and Sam alive so he and Kyle could get a redo when all of this was done.

"Get to the van! I'll cover you!"

Sam and Kyle ran past him as gunmen exited their vehicles. King had an AR pistol with a thirty-round magazine in his hands. He brought the Trijicon red dot optic up to his eye and pulled the trigger over and over again to lay down suppressive fire. He moved back and forth between targets to ensure all the gunmen had to take cover behind their doors. Then he heard his friends return the favor of cover fire from the van, so he turned to join them.

He watched as Lawson waved him forward from the driver's seat. King ran for the open side door and dove through onto the floorboard, sliding in beside the two captain's chairs that made up the second row. Kyle slammed the door shut, and Lawson hit the gas pedal. The van slid sideways off the road; then Lawson corrected it and sped away from the two vehicles King had just held at bay.

"Xander, we still have the plane at the airport," Sam said. "Let's get the hell out of this war zone and regroup when we can put things back to our advantage."

King wasn't expecting that. At no point when Sam had mentioned they were coming via private jet did he ever think of using the plane to escape.

Lawson beat King to it from the driver's seat. "You might get another shot at Ortega one day, but if you leave now, the next time you meet Scott Smith, you won't see him at all. He'll be hiding in his sniper perch, and they'll be burying you for real this time."

"Who the hell are you to chime in?" Sam said.

"I wouldn't be here without him, Sam," King said. "And he's right. Ortega's one thing, he's not leaving Mexico City, but Smith will follow me wherever I go until I'm dead. Or until one or more of you are."

Before Sam could answer, their minds were made up for them. The direction Lawson had to drive to get away from the gunmen was past the place where Scott Smith was staying. Before they ever even made it to the driveway, the passenger-side front tire exploded and the van slid out of control off to the left. King's figured Smith had just put a sniper round through the tire.

Lawson tried to keep the van from slamming into the apartment complex across the street, but the van was going too fast. When he turned the wheel back to the right, the top-heavy van tipped over and skidded on its side down the middle of the street. The van's momentum took them about fifty yards past Smith's hideout. The van slammed into more than one car before it finally came to a stop. It was lying on its side, the passenger doors trapped against the pavement, the undercarriage facing in the direction of the sniper. King had been thrown against the back passenger door, and the shattered glass from the windows showered all of them inside.

King ejected his magazine, pulled the spare from his pocket, and locked it in. He pulled the charging handle, then pulled himself up. He could hear the gunmen's vehicles pull up not too far from them.

"Kyle, pull the door handle and let it slide open!"

Kyle was held in the driver-side backseat by the seat belt.

"There's a sniper, X. You can't stick your head out!"

"They're about to start spraying the van with bullets. I have to hold them off!"

Kyle pulled handle on the van, and the automatic door slid back. A light came on inside the van. King's feet were now poking through the broken window on the street. Sam had pulled her knees to her chest to give him room.

"Jack, get the back door open. When I start shooting, you and Zhanna get out and take cover behind the van. But you have to be fast. When they start shooting, the rest of you make your way out!"

Jack didn't respond.

"Jack! You all right?"

"He's unconscious," Zhanna said. "But I think he's all right. I'll get door when you shoot."

"I'll be right behind you," Sam said.

"Toss me up an AR," Lawson said. "I'll help you hold them off."

King heard Lawson's window roll down. Everything was quiet except for the occasional horn from some impatient people now stuck in traffic. Zhanna handed Lawson an AR, and he was ready. King gave him a nod. King then placed his left foot on the side of the captain's chair, and it was enough to get his shoulders up out of the van. He immediately ducked back down into the van when a barrage of bullets began clanking against the undercarriage.

"Shit. They have us dead to rights!"

"I've got you," Lawson said. "On the count of three."

King looked over at Zhanna and Sam who had crawled to the back of the van. They were ready.

"Three ... Two ... One ..."

King raised up, leading with his AR above his head. He began pulling the trigger before he could even see the two trucks in the middle of the road. He heard Lawson shooting from the front, and he heard the clank of a sniper round hit the open back door, just missing both Sam and Zhanna. King wasn't sure if anyone had been hit, but at least two of his friends had made it out of the van. Kyle had unfastened his seat belt and was helping Jack, who was on his way back from unconsciousness.

King's AR pistol locked back. Kyle heard it and was already handing him a spare mag for his pistol and another for Lawson's. King reached around the front seat, and Lawson took possession. The return fire began from the men in the street.

"On my mark, Lawson," King said.

"Copy."

"Kyle, your turn," King said. "You think you can get Jack out?"

"I'll be fine," Jack murmured.

King looked down at Kyle. "I love you, brother. I'm sorry for the last two years."

King hadn't meant to say anything about it, but in between firing and watching Kyle help Jack, it just came out.

"Can we talk about this later?" Kyle said.

"Just wanted you to know."

Kyle nodded, then crawled over the back of the third row and readied himself to exit with Jack when King and Lawson commenced shooting. The inside of the van smelled like scorched metal and smoky sulfur. King was about to remind Kyle to grab some guns, but his friend was already stuffing his pockets and throwing straps over his shoulder. Jack was aware enough to grab for ammo. King removed his go bag and tossed it to the back.

"Fill that up. On my mark, boys. Ladies? Can you hear me?"

"We copy." Sam's voice carried through the walls of the van.

"Kyle and Jack are coming out. Stay behind the truck. Don't give Smith anything to aim at."

"Copy."

Luckily for the guys going out the back, the lift gate door was there to shelter them from the sniper. King knew that Smith would know this as well, so he would be fixed on King and Lawson.

"Lawson, don't poke anything out the window but the gun."

"Roger that."

King counted down. "Three . . . Two . . . One . . ." He was already pulling the trigger when he said "one." He knew he was firing in the general direction of the gunmen's vehicles, but he had no idea how close he and Lawson were to hitting the gunmen. Judging by the large amount of return fire, they clearly weren't hitting much.

"Go, Lawson. Make sure no one is coming up behind us."

Lawson stopped firing and King felt him move behind him for the back of the van. The easy part was finished. Everyone was out safely. The next part—getting out of the entire situation—would be much more difficult. They wouldn't have much to hide behind as they moved away from the van, and that would leave them open to the scope Smith was staring down at that very moment. King hoped the cars they'd hit while skidding to a stop were still close. Maybe that could be their way out.

Then came the sirens.

He'd narrowly been able to escape the presence of the police all day. Which had been quite the feat given the number of encounters he'd had with banging guns and exploding cars. As he crawled over the third row and the gunfire ceased out on the street, he was fairly certain his luck was about to run out.

One would usually think it better for an innocent man to be caught by the police rather than by the enemy's sniper round to the head. But in some parts of the world, those two things could be one in the same for the good guys.

37

The wailing sirens seemed to be coming at King and his friends from all 360 degrees. King stepped out of the back of the van where he was greeted by a cool breeze and the lunch-box-sized hand of Lawson Raines grabbing him by the shirt and pulling him around the corner to safety. The surrounding residential area just outside the tall buildings of the city were quiet except for the police cars coming. No more gunfire, and no real street noise at all since they had both sides of the road blocked. Crouched behind the overturned van, King and his crew were out of the sniper's sights.

"The gunmen just packed it up and pulled away," Sam said. "Could that mean they don't own all the cops?"

"It means we have to go too," Kyle said. "They won't own them all, but believe me when I tell you if there is one cop on their payroll, they'll find us."

"You all can go," King said as he replaced the magazine in his AR. "I can't let Smith out of here. He gets away now, we may never see him again."

"Isn't that a good thing, son?" Jack said.

"Apparently I have enough people in the world I gotta keep looking over my shoulder for. I don't need another one." King looked over at Lawson. "Besides, he needs to pay for what he did to Brittany McKinley."

"I came here to get the person who kidnapped Brittany," Lawson said. "I don't ever quit before the job is done. I'm ready."

The sirens were getting closer.

Kyle stepped toward Lawson. "We're all ready. That's not the point." Kyle looked over at King but pointed at Lawson. "Who the hell is this guy anyway?"

Lawson was unbothered by Kyle's bravado. "Police are closing in. It's now or never."

King looked over at Jack, his resident sniper. "You think Smith is still on his perch?"

"No. But I do things differently than kid killers. So you can't be sure."

King nodded. "Where's Zhanna?"

Jack motioned toward the six or so abandoned cars behind them. "She's staying low, checking for a getaway vehicle."

"Got one!" Zhanna said with a muffled voice. "White SUV!"

"Keep your heads down," King said. "Let's go."

King ducked down and moved in between the first two cars. After one more row of two cars, he saw the white SUV. He hurried over and opened the door. Zhanna had crawled into the front seat but was ducked down behind the steering wheel. She didn't know for sure that Scott Smith had a good enough look at her to shoot, but she wasn't taking any chances. Everyone else hurried inside the SUV.

Zhanna started it, backed up, then steered around the vehicles.

"Zhanna, this is too risky," King said. "Just turn around and we'll go up the back side of the house."

"He will get away. I have to at least run over his getaway motorcycle."

She stayed low in her seat as she made it past the overturned van, moving in the direction of where Smith had been staying. Then the first sniper round burst through the front windshield.

King was sitting diagonally behind the driver's seat on the passenger side. The spray of Zhanna's blood was warm on his face.

"Zhanna!" Jack shouted from the back.

The SUV sped forward as Zhanna's slumped body forced her foot down on the pedal. When her hand dropped from the steering wheel, the SUV turned right, away from Smith's house. Another round pierced glass, this time through the window of the seat behind the driver. Fortunately, the bullet went straight through the glass next to King. It couldn't have missed him by more than a couple of inches.

"Zhanna!" King heard Jack shout again.

King watched as Sam reached across the console for the steering wheel from the passenger seat. He saw red and blue lights flashing through the splintered front windshield. Then another round broke the glass in the back of the SUV. King turned around and saw that it had knocked Jack's hat right off his head. The SUV finally slammed into a car that had been abandoned earlier. Another round burrowed into the side of the SUV.

They were sitting ducks.

King grabbed the AR pistol that was hanging from the strap around his neck. He opened his door and stepped out.

"Stay down!" he told his friends.

He ducked under the window of the SUV and walked to the taillight. As police cars began screeching to a stop all around the cars in front of their crashed SUV, another sniper round hit the door on the other side. King brought the AR's red dot optic up to his eye, pivoted around the taillight, found the top window of Smith's hideout, and sent six rounds through. He pivoted back to cover.

"Everyone out of the vehicle with your hands up!" King heard a man with a Mexican accent speak through a megaphone. Though his mind was on laying cover fire for his team, he couldn't help but think it was odd that the officer wasn't speaking Spanish.

King pivoted once again and found the second upstairs window in his sights. He put six more rounds into the house. Since he'd started firing, there hadn't been another blast from the sniper rifle.

"Put the gun down and your hands behind your head! Now!"

Lawson climbed out of the back of the SUV. "That's it, King. We'd better hope your presidential connection is as strong as it sounded on the phone earlier." Then Lawson turned toward the front of the SUV. "We've got a gunshot victim! She needs help!"

King glanced back inside the SUV and saw Sam trying to keep the blood from leaking out of Zhanna's neck. He could see that her hands were covered. King's hand tightened around the grip of his gun. Zhanna was in bad shape. King was enraged.

"We have medical coming. But I need you to put down

your weapons and step away from the vehicle!" the policeman responded to Lawson.

"I need help here!" Sam shouted. "She's dying!"

Jack had crawled up through the SUV and was now trying to help Sam stop Zhanna from bleeding out. King didn't want to, but he already knew their attempts were futile. He felt the anger growing inside him. He looked over at Lawson, who had his hands clasped behind his head. Two police officers were approaching him, both with handcuffs at the ready.

Suddenly something familiar sounded off in the direction of Smith's hideout. It was unmistakable. King had owned a motorcycle his entire adult life and had always loved the sound when it first fired up. Scott Smith was about to make his getaway.

King watched Lawson glance to his left, in the direction of the motorcycle. The first police officer had just grabbed his right arm. Lawson glanced back at King, making sure King could see him. He gave King a nod. Before the officer could cuff Lawson's right wrist, the big man turned on the officer and pinned him against the SUV. King then realized what Lawson meant by saying he hoped his presidential connection was strong. It wasn't so the president could get them out of a Mexican prison; it was so the president could get Lawson out of prison for attacking the policemen to prevent them from stopping King from going after Scott Smith.

Few bonds are as strong as the ones formed in battle. Especially when someone lays their own life on the line for you or for the mission. King knew that for Lawson, going back to prison after spending ten years there already had to be a fear greater than dying. Yet Lawson stood in the officer's path anyway. Their bond had been forever forged in that moment. Now it was King's responsibility to make sure Lawson's sacrifice wasn't for nothing.

The second officer reached for his gun. Before King could move forward, Kyle was out the door with his feet on the ground. He'd kept the officer from pulling his gun on King by tackling the officer to the ground. Both policemen were contained. The path to their empty squad car had been cleared.

King heard the high-pitched whine of the motorcycle's engine racing off in the opposite direction. King ran for the police car, ignoring the other officers all standing outside their vehicles with their guns drawn, and jumped inside.

King threw the car in drive and mashed the gas pedal to the floor. He was going to run down Scott Smith no matter what it took. At least for trying to set King up and ruin his name but, most of all, for Brittany McKinley—and for Zhanna, one of his only friends in the world, who he was afraid was currently taking her last breaths.

38

Alexander King left a trail of smoke behind the stolen police car as he sped off into the night. The lights were still flashing on the roof, and King had no intention of shutting them off. He'd take every advantage he could get. On the radio, he could already hear the police reporting the stolen cruiser. As he swerved around a grouping of cars, he found the volume and shut it off. As he'd jumped in the police car, he'd tuned his ears to the sound of the motorcycle's engine. He never heard Smith throttle down, so he knew Smith hadn't slowed to take the first turn off the main road. So King tested the cruiser's torque as he surged straight ahead.

The motorcycle had a big advantage in traffic. It could fit into spaces that four-wheeled vehicles could not. But the flashing lights of the police car were a bit of an equalizer in that regard, because the traffic parted when they saw King in their rearview. King raced around cars at a red light and caught his first glimpse of Smith's back end. The motorcycle swerved right onto a side street, nearly clipping a car on its way.

King followed close behind.

The hardest part about catching Smith wasn't going to be stopping him. It was going to be stopping him without killing him. As much as King would like to just run him over, or jump out of the car and squeeze him by the neck until he was no longer breathing, King needed him alive. He needed to know why Smith was doing all of these things, and he needed to know either who was helping him or who was in charge. Not that Smith would give up that information easily, but King certainly wouldn't get any answers if Smith were dead. So he had to be careful.

King took each right and left turn that Smith took, doing his best to keep up with the speedy motorcycle. King could cut corners in a car that Smith couldn't, and that was helping to keep the gap small. Smith cut around two vehicles at a light. King wiggled his way around them and the oncoming traffic turning into his lane. He lost sight of the motorcycle as it sped away around the building on the corner. King was afraid he'd lost him.

When he finally made it around the traffic, his fear turned to elation as he saw a wall of cars up ahead, just beyond a cross street, and apparently Smith had cut it too close and been knocked off his bike. King sped forward then slid sideways to a stop, jumped out of the car, and put Smith in his sights.

"Don't touch that bike, Scott. I have no problem shooting you dead."

Smith was getting up to his feet. The motorcycle was about fifteen feet from him. The car that had taken him down sped off down a side street. King moved around his car door and walked forward with his gun squared on Smith's chest. There was nowhere for Smith to go.

"Hands up and stop walking."

Smith did as King asked.

King moved forward. He was only about ten feet away.

"Who sent you?" King couldn't wait any longer. He had to know.

Smith didn't speak.

King pulled the trigger and shot Smith in the right leg. "Who sent you?"

Smith collapsed to the ground, then slowly rose to his feet. "Does it really matter, King? The damage is done. You're done."

King moved the aim of the short-barreled AR from Smith's leg to his head. "You're the one who's done. Now it's just a matter of whether you survive me right now or you rot in prison. Doesn't matter to me either way."

Horns began sounding around them, as they were holding up traffic.

"Tell me who you're working with and I'll let you live," King said. He was now only a few feet away from Smith. Close enough that King could see the stubble of his beard, the missing index finger, and the fear of death in his eyes. He was about to talk.

"I tell you who I'm working with, you get me a deal," Smith said. "If you have any pull left, that is."

King thought of President Gibbons.

"You'll have to give someone up who's worth making a deal for. And don't worry about pull. I've still got plenty."

"Trust me," Smith grinned. "The people will care far more about who I give up than they'll care about me."

"All right. I can pull some strings. Get in the back of the car."

Smith put his hands above his head and took a step toward the police car. It was the last step he would ever take. Out of the cross street a black SUV came speeding through the light. It hit Smith so hard, it knocked him right out of his shoes. King could feel the hot wind of the SUV as it blew by him. King shouted "No!" as a knee-jerk reaction. He knew his chance of finding out who framed him might have just died right in front of him.

However, when two more SUVs pulled up, King quickly jumped back to reality realizing Smith getting hit was no accident. A few Mexican men piled out of the SUV that hit Smith, and also from the last SUV that had pulled up. About a half dozen of them in total. All of them were carrying semiautomatic rifles, and every one of them was pointed straight at King. Everyone's eyes seemed to be on the SUV in the middle. The driver stepped out and opened the back door. A man not much older than King emerged. His jet-black hair was slicked straight back. He was wearing a maroon suit with a white open-collar shirt. And his white smile glowed beneath his brown skin. King recognized Raúl Ortega immediately.

"Alexander King," Ortega said as he took a few steps toward King.

There was nowhere for King to go, and there were too many of them to fight.

"You mind putting the gun down?"

King lifted the strap over his shoulder and laid the AR on the ground. Even if he wanted to shoot, he'd be dead before he got them all. Beyond that, for some reason King got the immediate vibe that Ortega's interest in King might just be not to kill him. Behind King tires squealed against pavement. King looked back, and the white SUV he and his team had piled into after the van toppled over came swerving around the corner. Somehow his team had come for him.

Two of Ortega's men rushed in front of him to provide cover. The rest of his men readied their weapons. The white SUV slid to a stop, and Sam, Kyle, Jack, and Lawson all stepped out with guns drawn. King was caught in the middle, the only one standing without a weapon in his hands.

It wasn't his favorite place to be.

39

With streetlights glowing over the road, King felt like he had a spotlight on him the way he was alone in between Ortega's men and his own team. As if he were on stage. The problem was, this was no play, and no one was going to shout, "Scene!" so King could move from the danger he was in.

"You'd better have them put the guns down, King!" Ortega shouted, pushing through the two men trying to guard him.

"No way we're putting ours down until you do!" Kyle shouted.

On the left, one of Ortega's men stepped forward, poked his rifle forward, and shouted something in Spanish. King watched Lawson move his pistol to that man and shout. "Stand down!"

This could spiral fast if King didn't gain some control over the situation. He threw up both of his hands—one palm facing his team and the other facing Ortega and his men. "Stop! Everybody calm down."

"Calm down?" Kyle said. "These thugs have guns on you, X!"

King turned to face him. "I said calm down! Put the gun down, Kyle." Then he looked at everyone. "All of you. Put 'em down!"

Sam lowered her weapon. "You sure about this?"

King nodded. Begrudgingly, his team did as he asked. Then he turned back to Ortega. "Come on. Let's work something out here. You want something from me, or you would have killed me before you ever got out of your truck."

"Is that right?" Ortega said.

"Am I wrong?"

Ortega stared at King for a moment. Then he looked over at his men and waved his hand downward. They did as he asked and lowered their weapons. Ortega took a few steps toward King. His men fell in behind him. King felt his team move in closer.

"Mr. King, I have a . . . a proposition for you."

"I'm listening."

"Let's talk over here," Ortega said as he motioned toward the parking lot. "Let the people have their street back. My men will move your vehicles. Let's walk over here together."

King nodded and signaled for his team to follow. Ortega's men put Scott Smith's lifeless body in the back of one of the SUVs. In a matter of a minute, the entire twisted caravan was moved from the road to the parking lot of some sort of paycheck cashing business.

"Okay, now let's hear it," King said.

Ortega gave a crocodile grin. "As I'm sure you know by now, I have a *very* lucrative business here in Mexico City."

"Our definitions of *business* might be a little different. But I get your point."

"Maybe, but I make a lot of money and live a very nice life. I made a poor decision doing a deal with someone from your country, and I don't want things to change here because of it."

"Aside from the drugs you stashed at my home, what does that have to do with me?"

"Ah, see, this is my point," Ortega said as he smoothed back his hair. His men gathered around him once again. "I had nothing to do with those drugs at your home. But when I saw the report as you did, I realized I wasn't really a business partner to my new associate. I was simply part of the setup. Maybe even a victim of it myself."

"Would you like to tell me who this associate is?"

"I'm getting to that."

"Well, I don't have a lot of time," King said. "See, you aren't the only one who wants me. The police will be here any second."

"They don't want you either," Sam said from behind King.

King turned to face her. "I'm assuming that's how you were able to get here? They let you leave?"

"Yes," Sam said. "As soon as you left in the police car, the chief of police pulled up and explained how the President of the United States personally called the ambassador to make sure you were no longer considered a wanted man."

King turned back to Ortega. "Helps to have friends in high places."

Ortega folded his arms across his chest. "Which is precisely why we are talking now."

"A couple of hours ago you had one of my own in José turn on me. Now you want to talk? What changed?"

"You are still jumping to too many conclusions," Ortega

said, placing his hands on his hips. "I'm assuming while you were with José, he was pushing to have you take me out?"

"Yes, but that hardly means you didn't tell him to slant it that way."

"True, but let me ask you this. At what point did he turn on you?"

King looked to his left at Lawson while he searched his mind for what Ortega might be getting at.

Lawson reminded him. "When you decided killing Ortega was the long game. And you wanted to wait for backup."

King looked back at Ortega. "I wanted the laptop with the evidence of the doctored videos of me. José pushed to go after you."

"Then he left you for dead in your car," Ortega said.

"So what?" King said. "You arranged to have videos doctored of me kidnapping Brittany McKinley, and that set all of this in motion. Whether José was acting independent of you or not doesn't really matter. You started him down the path."

"It does matter, Mr. King. I only found out you were here in Mexico City when I watched the kidnapping video on television this morning like the rest of the world."

Hearing that surprised King.

"José put this entire thing together," Ortega continued. Then he pointed over at the SUV where his men had moved Smith's dead body. "That is why Scott Smith is lying dead in my truck and not you. He and José planned all of this. And yes, they did use my nephew to fake the videos." Ortega nodded to one of his men.

The man walked over and presented a closed briefcase. Ortega reached over, pushed the two chrome buttons, and the top popped open. Inside were eight fingers and two thumbs. Ortega looked back at King with a proud smile.

"My nephew has made his last video. His fingers are my gift to you."

"Charming," King said.

Then King was quiet as he processed. All along he'd just assumed Ortega was involved. All signs pointed in that direction. But flipping back through the entire day's events, he supposed there wasn't any absolute proof that Ortega himself had anything to do with the setup. People who worked for him certainly did. And as light traffic began to pass once again on the street beside them, that was where King's questions started.

"Then why meet with Scott Smith at the St. Regis hotel if you had nothing to do with this?"

"I had nothing to do with Scott Smith either. But he is one of the reasons that new associate of mine and I will no longer be discussing business. Smith blackmailed his way into a meeting with me at my hotel. He was trying to double dip. He was hired by my associate from the States, but he also wanted money from me. Smith threatened to pin everything that happened with you and this Brittany McKinley on me if I didn't pay him five million dollars. He said it could all easily be tied to you and me being partners. After he left, I thought about it, and he was right. He and José could easily make it look like I was involved. That's why Smith is dead."

"Okay," King said. "Even if I was to buy all of that. If all of that is true—you not planting the drugs, you not being involved in the fake videos, and you not putting José out to kill me—if all of those coincidences just so happen not to involve you, what about Brittany McKinley? You can explain those other things away because you weren't there, but I saw you, with my own eyes, taking Brittany into your building last night."

"You're right. I did. And this is where you need to understand who my new business associate was so what I'm about to tell you will make sense. It might blow your mind, but at least you will understand."

King looked at each of his team. He wanted to ask how Zhanna was doing, but it wasn't the time. King was trying to remain neutral so that he could determine whether or not he could believe Ortega. And as King looked back at Ortega, he couldn't help but smile. A lot of people in King's career of service to his country have told him they were going to shock him with a certain piece of information, but very few ever succeeded. King figured by that point, he'd just about seen it all.

"Okay then, Mr. Ortega," King said. "Wow me."

"Brittany McKinley was in my company last night because I took her from where Scott Smith was hiding her at the Marriott Hotel. As I'm sure you know by now, Smith was the one to kidnap her and bring her here from California."

"I do know that. What I don't understand is what any of this has to do with me. But before that, how would you even know that Brittany was here if you weren't involved with Smith, and why would you go out of your way to help Brittany, whom you don't know, for no reason? Not exactly the trait of a drug lord to help a stranger."

"Let me guess," Lawson interrupted. "Your new business associate."

Ortega pointed to Lawson and laughed. "Ah, smart man.

A good leader should be judged by the strength of those around him."

King wasn't amused. "How would your business partner have knowledge of Brittany McKinley being kidnapped, and why would they care if you saved her?"

"Because," Sam said as she stepped forward, "Ortega's business partner was Brittany McKinley's father."

40

King looked at Sam with a blank stare. He didn't have the piece of information Sam did in order to put what Ortega was saying together.

"You think Senator McKinley is behind all of this?" King said to Sam. Then he looked back at Ortega, and by the smirk on his face King knew Sam was right.

"She stole my punch line," Ortega said. "But at least she still blew your mind."

Ortega was right. This one had shocked King.

"It first crossed my mind when Dbie had mentioned he was the chairman of the FBI Oversight Committee," Sam said.

When the president had told King the same information, because it was McKinley's daughter who was taken, he hadn't given it a second thought. It was then that he realized, Senator McKinley had had his own daughter kidnapped to keep himself from looking guilty if things went sideways.

"Needless to say," Ortega said, "his plan of using his daughter to keep himself looking innocent *really* backfired."

King couldn't believe a father would put his child in harm's way like that.

"Sick bastard got what he deserved," Lawson said.

King turned toward Lawson. "You know him, Lawson. He capable of this?"

"I don't know him. I knew Brittany. Hiring me to find her must have been just another way of making it look like he'd do anything to get her back. Every one of us standing here was a pawn in his game."

King knew Lawson was right. But the last thing he didn't understand was why Senator McKinley had involved King. Regardless, King had to take working his way through all of the information one step at a time. And he had to start with the problem in front of him.

"Okay, Ortega. Now that we've played out your little show and you have my attention, you still haven't told me what you want from me. I'm hoping as you do, it will shed some light on why and how you got into bed with Senator McKinley in the first place."

"The how and the why of my business does not concern you. I get to keep those things to myself."

"Then how can you expect me to do something for you?"

"I'm hoping for some good faith, Mr. King. I could have killed you. I didn't. I could have let you continue to chase your tail about who is actually out to get you, but I didn't. You now know that a very powerful and influential man in your government is dirty. And I assure you, once you look into it, he is much dirtier than a small scheme to incriminate you."

"Don't act like you're doing me favors," King said. "You're doing this because McKinley can make it look like you were responsible for all of this too, and you want me to stop him. The minute Scott Smith shot Brittany, it made you look bad. It was Smith's way of leveraging you."

"Which didn't work in his favor, but yes. Which also helps you, King. Because I gave you McKinley, you can now go and prove you are innocent by showing he did all of this. Which also proves I had nothing to do with it, and that keeps the heat off me. I really don't understand the hesitation," Ortega said. Then he looked back at his men. "Am I missing something? Is this not a fair deal?" Then he gave a sweeping look at King's team. "You all see the win-win in this, right?"

"I see it, Ortega," King said. "I just don't make deals with scumbags who trade kids for money."

Ortega's men raised their guns. King's team responded by raising theirs. Ortega waved the men off, telling them to put down their guns. Then he smiled wide as he looked into King's eyes.

"No, Mr. King. You just decide who lives and who dies on your whim. And you're allowed to do so in the name of your country and its safety. You can hide behind that veil if you want, but you and I both know we aren't so different. I just get paid a lot more than you do to do bad things."

Years ago, a man like Ortega comparing himself to King would have sent King through the roof. But on more than one occasion, King had had the same thought. He understood where Ortega was coming from—and there was some truth to it—but they weren't the same. King would never take an innocent child from their family and sell them into a life of slavery. And he would never hook people on drugs for profit.

"Okay, Ortega, we're the same." King was sarcastic. "Whatever helps you sleep at night. All I care about now are two things. First, getting to the man responsible for Brittany McKinley's death and the shit situation I've been put in down here. The second is getting my team out of Mexico City safely. Now that you've divulged who's responsible, after we leave here in one piece, you can go back to your sinister business without interference from American agencies on one condition."

"I don't like conditions, Mr. King."

King took a step toward Ortega; they were almost nose to nose. "I don't give a damn. It happens on my condition, or an army comes down here for you next. Whether you kill me here or not."

"Okay," Ortega said. "I'll indulge you. What is it?"

"No more human trafficking."

Ortega looked up into the night sky. He gave no indication what his answer would be.

King continued. "I can stomach you pedaling drugs to adults who can make their own decisions about what they put in their own bodies. What I will not leave here knowing is that you are kidnapping innocent children to trade them to devils all around the world. I'll die where I stand before that happens."

"I wish I'd never taken that call from Senator McKinley," Ortega said, shaking his head. "Stupid mistakes are expensive."

"You've got plenty of money. Leave kids out of it."

"This is not an easy request. I have pipelines. People counting on me to make them a lot of money."

"The reason you kept me alive is because you know if I die, the cavalry comes," King said. "You heard Sam, the President himself called your ambassador to keep the police from coming for me. You don't think he'll send however many soldiers it takes down here for you if I die? You know that's a fact. And you know if I leave here, telling my people we're going to back off your operation, it will happen. But if you tell me you're through with the trafficking business, and I find out later you haven't kept your word, you know I'll be the one leading the soldiers down here to find you myself."

"I don't need to be threatened, Mr. King. Be careful the words you choose."

"And you be careful with the decision you make."

Ortega took a moment. King couldn't stand it any longer, and he looked back at Sam. He mouthed Zhanna's name to her. Sam just hung her head. A wave of sadness rushed over King. He didn't know for sure if Zhanna was dead, but by Sam's response, he knew she was at least at its doorstep.

"No more undercover agents like Mr. Ramirez?" Ortega finally said.

"No more undercover agents," King agreed.

"No more agents like you coming down here to sniff around?"

"I'll be the last," King said.

"Have a safe flight back to the States," Ortega said. "And I hope you don't let the senator make it to jail."

"He'll get what's coming to him. And you'll be able to see it on the news."

Ortega nodded. "I hope I never see you again, Mr. King."

"Ditto."

King turned back toward his team. He had just made Ortega some pretty big promises. And while he was sure he would be able to keep his word, that didn't mean there weren't workarounds. But as long as Raúl Ortega stayed away from trafficking children, King didn't really give a damn what happened to him.

The only things on King's mind now were Zhanna and getting a crack at Senator McKinley. But as he watched Lawson Raines climb into the driver's seat of the SUV, he figured he first might have to fight Lawson to see who got dibs on McKinley.

41

T hree Days Later

ALEXANDER KING WAS happy to be back Stateside. Though he'd rather be at his home in Kentucky, looking out over the rolling hills, instead of his view of the Potomac from Director Lucas's office in Langley, he still had important business to tend to. Over the last seventy-two hours, Dbie, Sam, Lawson's partner, Cassie, and more than a dozen other agents at the CIA had been doing a deep dive into Senator Terry McKinley's recent past. It never ceased to amaze King how dirty some seemingly squeaky-clean people can be. Senator McKinley was a full-on mud pit.

No one other than King's team, Director Lucas, and the President knew that King had made it back from Mexico City alive. That's why when McKinley was escorted into

Director Lucas's office, he nearly fell over in shock when he saw King.

King turned from the window to face him. "What's wrong, Senator? You look like you've seen a ghost."

Lucas walked in behind McKinley, and McKinley turned toward him immediately. His face was beet red, and King could have sworn he saw foam in the corner of his mouth. "What is going on here, Robert? I buried my daughter this morning. And you have the nerve to bring me here with him?"

King took a few steps across the office toward McKinley. "I'm going to talk now, Senator. I advise you to listen and keep your mouth shut."

"Or what?"

King answered with a right hand to McKinley's jaw. McKinley dropped to the floor, and with shock on his face he looked up at Director Lucas. "Don't just stand there, Robert! Arrest this man!"

Director Lucas turned his back to McKinley and looked out the window. Then Lawson Raines walked into the room. Lucas wasn't happy about King inviting him along, but King felt Lawson deserved to see the takedown of the monster who not only got Brittany killed but nearly got Lawson killed as well by involving him in the entire mess.

"You going to take my advice now and listen?" King said. He nodded to the two agents behind McKinley to help him back to his feet. McKinley wiped the blood from his mouth and straightened his navy sport coat. But he didn't speak. McKinley watched Lawson as he walked around them and took a seat just a couple of feet away.

"The hell's he doing here? What are both of you doing

here?" McKinley looked at King. "You both are the reason my daughter is dead!"

King's voice was calm. "I'm glad you brought up Brittany. I honestly don't think in all of this that you meant to get your own daughter killed. But stupid is painful. And you made a lot of dumb decisions. I obviously didn't know Brittany long, but what little I did, I could tell she was smart and a good kid."

King could see the pain behind McKinley's eyes. It was either that or worry for what King was about to expose.

"As I'm sure you know by me standing here in front of you, and Robert letting me have a few minutes with you, we know everything."

King watched as the senator's face went from red to a pale shade of gray.

"You don't have shit on me, because there's nothing to have. Robert!"

King gave him a solid right hand to the gut.

"I said no talking. Keep it that way until I ask you a question."

McKinley took in a deep breath as he recovered.

King continued. "We know about your connection to Jimenez in Southern California. And that you've been using your own FBI special task force to shield him and his drug business. After we brought in Agent Daniel Wilson, the head of your little covert task force, he cooperated in naming you. And he had been keeping proof along the way in case things ever went sideways."

"Bullshit. I don't even know who you're talking about!" McKinley couldn't help himself.

King feigned like he was going to hit him, and McKinley

flinched so hard he almost fell over. King looked over at Director Lucas.

"This is embarrassing," King said to Lucas.

Robert shrugged, then looked at his watch. Lawson was stone-faced in his chair.

"Now to the really grimy stuff," King said. "Agent Wilson also gave us another name. Walker Reed. Mean anything to you?"

"Never heard of him," McKinley said.

"Yeah, I thought you might say that."

King pulled a small remote from his pocket, aimed it at the television, and pressed play. Senator McKinley appeared immediately. The video was shot from across a street. McKinley walked up to a man who stopped and took possession of the briefcase McKinley handed to him. They both turned to walk away at the same time, and King pressed pause. Both faces in the video were easy to recognize.

"You gonna keep making me do this?" King said.

McKinley didn't speak, but his shoulders slumped. He knew he was defeated.

"Okay. That was Walker Reed in that video with you. And the briefcase you handed him was full of money." King pressed another button, and a still image appeared of an open briefcase full of cash. "Agent Wilson knew a day like this might come since you were paying him to keep everyone from knowing you were stepping into the human trafficking business. Which is exactly what Walker Reed is wanted for. And Walker Reed just so happened to supply Raúl Ortega with these kidnapped bodies for the pleasure of the rich and famous all over the Southern Hemisphere. The same Raúl Ortega you began dealing with just a few weeks ago yourself when Ortega wanted to cut out the middle man in Walker Reed."

"Robert," McKinley said, "you really believe this story he's telling to cover his own ass? He did this! He took Brittany! Arrest him!"

King hit another button on the remote. A dark photo of the back of a car came into view on the TV.

"That's you on the right, as you can see," King said. "And the man on the left? You want to tell me or shall I continue to do the honors?"

McKinley looked from the television back to King. He knew what was coming. And the pain King thought he saw a moment ago looked a whole lot more like rage now.

"Fine," King said. "That is you making a deal with the man who shot your daughter in the head with a sniper round, Scott Smith. Scott has been on your payroll the longest, hasn't he?"

The rage was building on McKinley's face.

"Scott was the most difficult for us to get information on. But the President helped us out with that. He let us have access to redacted files, which led to Smith's old navy commanders, which led to stories of Smith as a head case, which was then corroborated by the men who'd served with him. When you ran into him at one of your rallies, you saw a lost soldier in need of a mission, and he became your go-between on all of these deals. Your right-hand man, you could say. That pretty much how it happened?"

McKinley looked like he was about to explode.

"It was Smith who used my passport to frame me at John Wayne Airport in Orange County. He then used your own human trafficking connections to kidnap your daughter and take her to Mexico. What you didn't count on was Raúl Ortega, a notorious scumbag, being smarter than you. And that was ultimately the reason your daughter died. Ortega took your daughter from Smith when he was meeting with an old navy buddy, and that is when everything unraveled. Your right-hand man turned on you. He knew once he had lost Brittany, you would turn on him. So he acted first. It was when he and his old buddy José Ramirez got greedy that your criminal acts turned into the death of your daughter."

King paused for a minute to let it all sink in.

"Both Smith and José knew I had money," King continued. "They knew you had money. They were going to either hold Brittany for ransom to get money from you, or bribe me for the information they had that could exonerate me by incriminating you. Whichever came first."

King looked over at Lawson.

"When your other plan to cover your tracks came into the picture and Smith saw Lawson here—whom I don't believe he knew you'd hired—he panicked and went with option B, blackmailing me, and put a quarter-sized hole in your daughter's head."

McKinley jerked forward, but the two agents caught him. King walked away toward the window.

"After finding all of this information," King said, "and clearly showing that you were responsible for all these terrible things, the only thing I couldn't understand, besides why would a man get into these kinds of criminal activities in the first place, was what in the hell did it have to do with me? I mean, you weren't even supposed to know I was alive."

King turned back toward McKinley. "Then it hit me. I remember sitting in my flat a while back in London watching the news announcing who would be running for President against the favorite, Bob Gibbons. I didn't remember them talking about you, because it was John Forester who was running for President. Senator Terry McKinley from California was merely his running mate. Senator, are you telling me that your spiral into all of this madness was because I foiled Husaam and Saajid Hammoud's attempt to get your running mate, John Forester, into office? You did all of this because my actions kept you from becoming Vice President?

"And then most likely President after that," McKinley added. "I would have eventually run the most powerful nation in the world. Gone down in history. If you just would have been dead like you were supposed to be."

"That's what you have to say? After all I've brought forward, your response is about a political position that you never had?"

"Not *a* political position," McKinley said. "*The* political position. Rigging the election so Bobby Gibbons could win was all the Deep State's plan. There was no Saajid Hammoud. He was a puppet like everyone else, to grab control of the most powerful country in the world. I had a line to it, and their puppet—*you*—ruined it!"

"Deep State conspiracy theories? You really have lost it, McKinley." King looked over at Director Lucas. "I guess you can add *nut job* as another adjective to describe this wacko." He looked back to McKinley. "I can't believe California voted you in for senator again. I hate what happened to your daughter, McKinley, but at least you're getting what you deserve."

For an older man, McKinley moved pretty fast. He jumped forward for King, but before King could put up his hands for a fight, a blur went by on King's right. It was as if Lawson's legs were on springs; that's how fast he made it to McKinley. Before King knew it, McKinley's feet were off the floor and he was flying through the air. McKinley went crashing through the mahogany coffee table, and before he could even roll over, Lawson was on top of him. King could hear the smacking thuds of Lawson's fists against McKinley's head. He knew from recent experience how bad those hurt.

"Get him off him, for God's sake!" Director Lucas shouted as he rushed over. "He's gonna kill him!"

One of the agents grabbed for Lawson's arm, but Lawson flung the agent back like he was made of paper.

"Don't just stand there!" Robert looked at King and shouted again. "Stop him!"

King didn't want to stop him. But he also didn't want Lawson going back to prison. King rushed over and lifted Lawson up from under his arms. When Lawson turned and pushed King back, his eyes were glazed over. He realized it was King he'd pushed; he looked down at the bloodied senator, chest heaving, then walked out the door. McKinley moaned in pain. King had accomplished what he wanted. He nodded a thank-you to Director Lucas for giving him the opportunity.

Then King had a thought. "Robert, there's still one thing left I don't understand."

"How McKinley knew you were alive?"

"Exactly. Only a few people know. How'd that happen?"

"I've been looking into it, but I don't know yet."

"Guess it doesn't matter now. The whole world knows I'm alive." King walked toward the door. "See you in a few?"

"I'll be there."

King checked his phone for the time. He was running behind. Unfortunately for him, the day ahead was only going to get worse. As he walked down the hall at Langley, one name came to mind who knew he was alive, and she wasn't part of the agency or on King's team. Bentley Martin. There was no way he would ever find out if Bentley stoked the senator's flames to go after King. With knowledge that King was alive, there was no way to set a trap to find out. King figured the girl who'd fooled him back in London was going to come to mind often until he finally saw her again. And he knew one day he would.

For now, though, he had even worse things to take care of.

42

Director Lucas had one of his agents give King a ride. The agent let King out at the entrance to his destination, and for a few minutes King found himself wandering around row after row of white marble headstones at Arlington National Cemetery. He had hoped that what happened earlier in Director Lucas's office would ease the sting of what was coming, but King hadn't felt such sorrow since losing his mother all those years ago.

In the distance he saw the circular white stone structure of the Memorial Amphitheater almost glowing against the bright blue sky. It was surrounded by green rolling hills that were filled with fallen soldiers who had made the ultimate sacrifice for their county and its freedoms. Though he was anything but joyful at that moment, King was happy that his friend Zhanna was going to be laid to rest in such hallowed grounds.

King wasn't naive. He knew who he was and what he did for a living. And he'd always known that if he did it long enough, he would lose someone he loved. That knowledge hadn't helped ease the pain of losing his Russian friend at all. She didn't have any family. She had no ties to her own country and no one else alive who could give her the burial she deserved. And while King knew nothing could make up for her loss, knowing she was getting a full US military funeral was at least a way to honor what she'd done for King and for the United States of America.

As he stood there in the glowing sun, with the glory of all the beautiful souls all around him who'd given to his country, he took a knee and observed a quiet moment. He wanted to use the energy of those around him to give him strength to carry on in their footsteps. A breeze rustled through the trees. A few birds sang to each other in the distance. And King felt a hand on his shoulder. When he rose to his feet, he saw the face of his old friend, and emotion overwhelmed him.

King wrapped Kyle in a hug, and the two of them cried. Tears for Zhanna. Tears for the two years they'd lost from each other's lives because of the things they had to do for their country. It was never easy, but neither of them ever thought it wasn't worth it. And it was in that moment that King's sadness turned into appreciation. We can never measure life by what we've lost, but instead by the moments we've yet to live. With Kyle's arms wrapped around him, he made the decision that he wasn't going to waste another minute of his life missing the opportunities to make memories with those he loved. No matter the consequences going forward.

King pulled back and took Kyle in. He hadn't changed a bit. His dark hair was still fixed in the same brushed-over style, his brown eyes still full of energy, and his square jaw stubbled as always.

"I'm not crying, you're crying," Kyle said through tears.

They both had a much-needed laugh.

"I'm sorry, Kyle." King ended his smile and squinted his eyes. "I made the decision I thought was best for your safety and—"

"I get it," Kyle interrupted. "I didn't at first. And I was pissed. But I know you. And I know you would never steer clear of my life if you didn't think it was life or death."

"It won't happen again."

"That's all that matters now."

Sam walked up. "You boys kiss and make up? Because we need to get over to the grave site."

"We're good," Kyle said as he put his arm around King.

"Good. Because Zhanna wouldn't want the two of you to stay angry. She rather enjoyed the cocky banter I've so grown to hate."

Sam gave them a wink and then cuddled up under King's arm. The three of them walked quietly to the last place any of them wanted to go.

43

Zhanna's send-off was no spectacle. There weren't a lot of people gathered around her casket, but some important people did show up to pay respects, and that meant a lot to King. The main VIP being the President himself. There was normally a long wait to have someone buried at Arlington. The President not only skipped the line for Zhanna, but he made it possible entirely. Arlington was reserved for US soldiers, which technically Zhanna wasn't, but he made sure she was recognized as one like she deserved. And he didn't skimp on ceremony. There was a casket team, a firing party, and a bugler all on hand to see her burial done properly. King gave Bobby a nod as he walked forward and laid a single white rose atop her cherrywood casket. King had chosen that type of wood to symbolize her red hair.

"Ladies and gentlemen," the chaplain said. "Coworker and friend of Ms. Dragov, Alexander King, would like to say a few words."

King nodded a thank-you to the chaplain. Then he took

a moment to look over the few who had gathered. There was of course Sam, Kyle, and Jack. Then he saw Lawson Raines with his arm around his blonde-haired daughter, Lexi. Lexi reminded King of his niece, Kaley. Lawson had flown his partner, Cassie, and Lexi there to pay respects to the woman who'd helped Lawson get out of Mexico City alive. On down the line of people, there were a few higher-ups in the CIA, including Director Lucas, and then of course the President and his wife, Beth.

King looked down at the casket and shook his head. He couldn't believe such a vibrant woman was gone. His heart longed to hear that Russian accent one last time. He looked up at Kyle and Sam for support. Both of them nodded and gave him a smile.

"I will *never* forget the first time I met Zhanna Dragov. My team had just arrived in Tuscany, Italy. We were regrouping before we went after Russian crime boss Vitalii Dragov. That's right, we were going after Zhanna's father. I remember hating her before I ever even met her because of who her father was. I was not happy at all that Sam had set it up. But when I saw Zhanna walk down out of that heli-copter . . ." King looked over at Kyle and gave him a wink. King couldn't help but laugh. "I have to tell you, she was hard to hate. Am I right, Kyle?"

Kyle nodded and wiped away a tear as he laughed.

"Kyle was in love at first sight, let me tell you."

King watched Sam give Kyle a playful elbow to the ribs as she smiled.

"Zhanna, as you all know, was a one-of-a-kind beauty. That fiery-red hair and those emerald-green eyes were enough to make anyone stop and take notice. And though it was the last thing I wanted to do at the time, I couldn't help but be mesmerized. But I'm going to tell you right now, as beautiful as Zhanna was on the outside, that was no match for the fire she had inside her to fight for what was right in the world. Even when that meant going up against her own father. And after we took care of business in Moscow, that flame never wavered on all the other missions we carried out. I can't tell you how many times that wonderful woman saved my life and the lives of my dearest friends."

King had to pause for a moment to let the rising emotion settle. Then he switched gears.

"There are a lot of important qualities a soldier, or an operator, has to have to do the things that Zhanna did for this country. You have to be smart, you have to be strong, and of course you have to be brave. But what you need most of all—the one quality that can often times beat all the others I mentioned put together—is heart. When your mind is telling you that you can't do something, or that something is too dangerous—when your brain screams at you not to go around that next corner because death will be staring you in the face—that's when the differentiator comes into play. And the only thing that can shut those instincts off, the ones screaming at you to turn and run, is when your heart wants to get the job done more than anything else. And Zhanna Dragov had the heart of ten men and women. So when you walk out of here today, I want all of you to do something for Zhanna. Live life with passion, as she did. Do the things you know need to be done, even when the consequences might lead you here." He pointed at the casket. "That's how you make a difference in this world, and Zhanna Dragov made a big damn difference, because she had an amazing heart."

King bent over and kissed the top of Zhanna's casket. It

was time to let her rest in peace. Kyle, Sam, and Jack walked around and did the same. Then the rest in attendance left a rose for Zhanna to take to her grave. King and his team walked out together with Lawson and his crew.

"Thanks for saying those words for her, son," Jack said. "You did real good."

"Thanks, Jack."

Lawson and his two ladies walked over.

"It was nice to meet you, Lexi," King said, shaking her hand. "You should be very proud of your father. He might be the toughest guy I know."

"Yeah, I think I'll keep him." Lexi smiled and hooked her arm around Lawson's.

King looked to Cassie. It was his first time meeting her. She was fit, with shoulder-length blonde hair and pale skin. "Thank you for helping out with research. I really appreciate it," he said, shaking her hand.

"I'm sorry about your friend."

"Thank you." King smiled. "Lawson tells me you and I are a lot alike. I'm not sure that's fair to you, but I do believe it means you're a lot of fun at parties."

"Oh brother," Sam said from behind him.

They all shared a laugh. King reached out his hand for Lawson. Lawson shook it with the power you would expect from someone his size. He was the type of guy who never knew his own strength. King was glad he didn't actually end up being an enemy.

"Lawson. We started out pretty rough, my friend. But now I trust you with my life."

"Same. And sorry about Zhanna. I know how fond of her you all were. Glad I got to meet her."

King nodded. He appreciated his new friend. "So, what's next for you?"

"Back to Orange County," Lawson said. "Apparently there was a local girl kidnapped last night. I've been given the call."

"The bad guys never sleep."

"Then neither will we," Lawson said.

"Listen, I know you have your own thing going in California, but I can always use someone like you."

"Hanging out with you is dangerous," Lawson said with a smile. "So I'd better stick to investigating."

King smiled back. "I hear you."

"That said, if you're ever in need, I won't leave you hanging."

"Thanks, brother. Get home safe."

Lawson, Lexi, and Cassie walked away, leaving Sam, Kyle, and Jack with King.

"Well, I'll say it again, I'm real proud of ya, son," Jack said. "You got her a proper burial. She deserved it."

"Yes she did . . ." King trailed off as he looked up at the sky and took a deep breath. "But she didn't deserve to die. And the only reason she did was because of me and the situation I was put in by the CIA just to run some recon mission."

Everyone nodded.

"That shit ain't happening again," King said.

"I like where this is going," Sam said.

"The next time we are caught in a bad situation, it's going to be on our terms. We've earned our right to pick and choose what the hell we want to fight for and the situations we want to be in."

"We're going out on our own?" Kyle said.

"We're going out on our own," King confirmed. "I've already talked it over with President Gibbons. He's going to smooth it over with Director Lucas."

"Finally," Sam said. "Maybe some good can come out of these terrible last few days."

"Well," Jack said, "unless one of you's is left for dead again, I'm goin' back to retirement."

"We'll miss you, old man. But thank you." King gave him a hug.

"Keep in touch now," Jack said.

"Will do." Then the cowboy walked off to head back to his farm where he belonged.

"When do we start?" Kyle said.

"Not sure, but I'm going home to Kentucky first," King said with a sigh. "I've got one more surprise for two very special ladies."

"Your sister and your niece might both have heart attacks when you show up on their front door," Kyle said.

"They might," King said. "Then can we meet back at my house tonight? Throw a celebration for Zhanna instead of all this sad stuff?"

"I think she'd want us to get proper drunk in her honor," Sam said.

"I agree," Kyle said. "We'll see you tonight. We have a lot to catch up on."

"Two years' worth," King said.

As the three of them left Arlington National Cemetery, King had mixed emotions. Burying a friend was never easy. However, with the new lease on an actual life he was walking toward, he couldn't help but feel excited. He missed his family. He missed his home. And he missed making memories with his friends that didn't have to do with other people's blood.

In one week's time King had gone from the most wanted man in the world to maybe the most free he'd ever felt. And it felt damn good.

POWER MOVE
Book 4 in the Alexander King series.

PRE-ORDER TODAY!

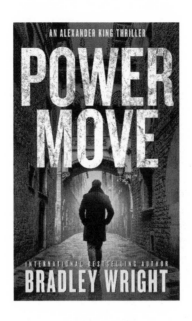

POWER MOVE
by
Bradley Wright

Book 4 in the Alexander King series.
Coming Summer 2021

ACKNOWLEDGMENTS

First and foremost, I want to thank you, the reader. I love what I do, and no matter how many people help me along the way, none of it would be possible if you weren't turning the pages.

To my family and friends. Thank you for always being there with mountains of support. You all make it easy to dream, and those dreams are what make it into these books. Without you, no fun would be had, much less novels be written.

To my advanced reader team. You continue to help make everything I do better. You all have become friends, and I thank you for catching those last few sneaky typos, and always letting me know when something isn't good enough. Alexander appreciates you, and so do I.

About the Author

Bradley Wright is the international bestselling author of action-thrillers. Most Wanted is his fifteenth novel. Bradley lives with his family in Lexington, Kentucky. He has always been a fan of great stories, whether it be a song, a movie, a novel, or a binge-worthy television series. Bradley loves interacting with readers on Facebook, Twitter, and via email.

Join the online family:
www.bradleywrightauthor.com
info@bradleywrightauthor.com

Made in the USA
Las Vegas, NV
12 August 2021